THE
LAST OUTLAW

Other books by Stone Wallace:

Denim Ryder
Montana Dawn

THE
LAST OUTLAW

•

Stone Wallace

AVALON BOOKS
NEW YORK

Published by Avalon Books,
an imprint of Thomas Bouregy & Co., Inc.
160 Madison Avenue, New York, NY 10016

Library of Congress Cataloging-in-Publication Data

Wallace, Stone, 1957–
 The last outlaw / Stone Wallace.
  p. cm.
 ISBN 978-0-8034-7665-3
 I. Title.
 PR9199.4.W3424L37 2011
 813'.6—dc22

                              2010046216

PRINTED IN THE UNITED STATES OF AMERICA
ON ACID-FREE PAPER
BY RR DONNELLEY, BLOOMSBURG, PENNSYLVANIA

*Dedicated with appreciation to my amigos Don and
Jacqui Tirschmann, whose friendship and generosity helped
smooth over some rough trails*

Author's Note

While the story of *The Last Outlaw* takes place in the beautiful state of Wyoming in the 1800s, most of the towns and locations described within are fictional.

No, I think it taught me to be independent and never expect a handout and never wait for anybody to hand you anything in any aspect of my life.

—Jesse James (1847–1882)

Prologue

Cash McCall sprinkled the last bit of smoking tobacco from his pouch onto thin rolling paper and carefully built a cigarette. He struck a match against his thumbnail and lit it, inhaling deeply and blowing out smoothly a fine stream of smoke. He watched the smoke drift upward before dissipating into clouds as transparent as his future.

He looked casually at his pocket watch. The gold-inlaid numerals told him that it was just after 1:00 A.M. Not that it made any difference. They were just numbers on a dial. Time had no meaning for him anymore. It never really had, except when he was counting away the minutes in prison. Years, months, weeks—even days. All held no meaning. Time behind bars was measured only in minutes. Long, endless minutes where each pass of the hand was a reminder of a life wasting away.

When he regarded time at all, it was as an enemy.

As the minutes slowly ticked by, Cash's rheumy eyes once more took in his dreary surroundings: a small, under-lit hotel room with cheap and sparse furnishings. A ratty upholstered chair upon which he was seated, plain wood table that creaked on an unbalanced leg, a dresser with a cracked rectangular mirror perched atop it, a nightstand with a low-burning kerosene lamp, and a bed with the sheets carelessly strewn about. He observed each of these items with a resigned detachment. Only the late-night shadows, creeping into the room through the thin fabric of the curtains and casting malevolent images across the far wall, seemed to arouse his interest. In these final moments he seemed to realize that he,

1

too, had become a shadow. No depth, little substance, and soon to be forgotten, fading into the night.

His cigarette was finished, and he mashed the butt into the worn surface of the table. He considered the half-empty bottle of whiskey that stood before him and gulped back a big swig, the liquor dribbling carelessly down the corners of his mouth. He moved to put the whiskey down, then drew back and impulsively took another swallow. He wasn't really drunk, though he debated whether he wanted to be. Perhaps it would somehow drown out the oppressive silence that permeated the room. A grim, unrelenting quiet that he was unable to ignore even with the persistent chattering of incomprehensible thoughts.

Finally Cash stood up, and his movement suddenly intensified the potent effects of the liquor. He swayed uncertainly for a moment until he could steady himself. He moved from the chair and walked over to the window, parting the curtains slightly and peering out at the rain that had begun to bead against the filmy glass, glistening translucently. After several moments he turned and moved away from the window—his boot suddenly striking something soft, vulnerable to the impact. Something out of place in the stark harshness of the room.

His gaze slid down to the floor to the small outstretched hand that lay below him. He regarded the hand and the curled fingers that had once tenderly caressed him. His eyes traveled the path of the arm to the body of a woman, sprawled motionlessly on the area rug.

Cash observed her raven-haired, supine form with a stare as blank as his remembrances. And perhaps it was better that way. For in just moments all emotion had drained from him. It was how it had to be. Still, that trace of human feeling that remained in him urged Cash to lower to a crouch and brush aside the strands of hair that had fallen across her face and once more touch the soft, warm skin. His expression stayed vacant as he laid gentle fingers against her cheek, sliding them toward her slightly parted lips.

He said nothing, just continued to observe the woman in the eerie stillness of the room. Finally he straightened to his feet, experiencing another rush of dizziness. Luckily, he recovered quickly.

Cash sighed, and the faint sound echoed throughout the room, shattering the quiet. He walked the few steps back to the table and reached for the Colt .44 he'd placed there. He spun open the cylinder and checked the chambers. Four bullets, just as he'd known. For one crazy second he'd hoped that his odds would be improved. That he'd miscounted . . . or that by some divine intervention those empty chambers might be filled.

But four chances would be all he was given. He had to score on each one, and even then he knew he was a dead man. He snapped the cylinder closed and hefted the revolver. It felt strangely foreign to him, and at the same time a wave of sickness not attributable to the alcohol he'd consumed coursed through his body. He slid the Colt into his holster, eager to be rid of its cold, unyielding touch if only for a few moments. He saw no point in concealing the gun, even if he could. They knew he would be armed.

He moved over to the dresser and regarded his reflection in the broken glass of the mirror. Even in the faded light he could see that his complexion was pale and wan, his face marked with lines that belied his twenty-eight years. Allowing himself one moment of vanity, he moistened his fingertips with the little bit of saliva he was able to draw and ran them through his coarse black hair, smoothing the tousled locks back over his forehead.

He was ready.

As he left the room, he brought himself to take another look at the woman lying on the floor. He was thankful that she would be spared these next horrible moments.

He used the key to lock the door behind him and proceeded down the narrow corridor with its stink of stale tobacco and hint of old whiskey. There were four rooms along this floor, but not a sound emanated from within any of them. He approached the staircase that would take him down to the main floor—and he hesitated. He felt alone. As alone as he had ever been in his life. Alone, as he saw it, for the last time.

As he slowly descended the carpeted steps of the staircase, the old material muting the footfalls of his boots, his final companion would be his thoughts, clearing of their jumble and beginning to assume a cohesive pattern that did not make his short journey any easier. He once remembered hearing that in the final moments of one's life the whole of a person's earthly existence passed before him. Cash's first clear moment of consciousness was that he was born in a run-down hotel and was now preparing to die in one. The irony was not lost on him.

And then, perhaps without really wanting to, he reflected on the events that had brought him to this moment of destiny. . . .

Chapter One

. . . He remembered the date: September 1, 1885.

That was the day Cash McCall stepped a free man from the high walls of the Territorial Prison at Bennetsville. It should have been one of the better moments in a misspent life.

But it wasn't. Not by a long shot. Truth be told, he was bitter and mean-mad at the world. Prison had been a cruel and harsh experience, and even the good behavior he had tried to observe made little difference when it came to the brutality of the guards. The Territorial Prison at Bennetsville was one of the most feared penal institutions in the West, whose sole purpose was to break incorrigibles, among which Cash McCall had found himself numbered. The system they employed was simple: if a hard case wasn't reduced to a whimpering pile of jelly within the first month, the guards were reprimanded for not doing their job. Every technique they used was intended to break the spirit, if not the body, of the offender. The prisoners were treated like animals, forced to endure backbreaking labor under the harsh glow of the sun all day, with little water or nourishment to help keep up their strength—and not one of the inmates daring to slow his pace or become ill lest he suffer even sterner punishment through a beating or forfeiture of the evening meal. They were kept in leg irons most of the time and made to wear stinking prison issue that clung to their bodies with their own sweat, clothing that was changed only once a week.

The mortality rate was high behind those walls. The filth the men were forced to live in contributed to it. Cramped cells that were shared with all sorts of sickness-breeding vermin. Hardly any medical care was available to treat the many whose bodies had become wracked with disease.

There was little interest in redemption behind those walls. Bodies could be carted out and buried with a lot less effort, at least from the guards. In addition to their other work duties, randomly chosen prisoners broke ground for plenty of graves.

It didn't take Cash long to recognize that he had taken the road straight to perdition.

He reminded himself that it was his own doing that had brought him to this misery. The details remained clear in his brain. Through all six years of his imprisonment each event was as vivid as if it had happened yesterday. . . .

His partner had said it was sure to be an easy and profitable job, and like the damn fool Cash reckoned he was born to be, he fell into his pal's smooth-talking trap and went along with his plan.

His partner's name was Steve Reno. And that's what most everyone called him. But because Steve had a great conceit and wanted to be remembered in history books, he'd tagged a more colorful moniker onto himself, one that he hoped would be written up by newspapermen always looking for a way to romanticize outlaws to the reading public. He called himself The Whiskey Kid, which was as unlikely a handle for Steve Reno as one could imagine. The Whiskey Kid suggested someone down and dirty in his appearance, not to mention careless and sloppy in manner, and, whatever his other faults, Steve never gave that impression. He was usually polite in nature and always mighty particular about the way he looked, down to the slightest detail.

The pair had strolled into the Hensford bank just before closing on a Friday, after the area farmers had deposited the cash from their harvests and the other customers had cleared out. Steve Reno's timing was perfect, as all the two men encountered were the bank president, seated in his open office off to the side, preoccupied with paperwork, and the two tellers standing behind their wickets, likewise busy adding up the money from their cash drawers before placing it in the safe.

Both men wore wide-brimmed Stetsons pulled low, shadowing the upper portion of their faces. Steve could not resist throwing Cash a confident smirk before he walked over to one of the wickets while his partner held back and tried not to look as suspicious as he felt. Cash waited until Steve had the teller's attention before he drew the kerchief up over the lower half of his face and pulled his six-shooter, turning it toward the bank manager.

Steve already had his own dark kerchief up, stepping back a few feet and holding both of his Colts at the ready, one aimed at each of the tellers. He didn't speak a word to either, but that was unnecessary, as his intention was clear. By now Cash had the manager's full attention, and as the uncertain man started to rise from behind his desk, Cash waved the barrel of his revolver in a gesture that told him to move away from his office, slowly and with hands raised high, and walk out onto the floor. The manager obliged without argument.

Steve supervised the collection. The tellers had already started pulling out the rest of the cash from their drawers and piling it on the counter. Once they were done, Steve gestured for them to join the manager on the floor, where Cash could watch them while Steve scooped up the bills and deposited the stacks of money into a cloth sack.

Cash couldn't deny he was nervous the whole time, trying not to be fidgety with his weapon . . . but he was also mighty impressed by how smoothly the procedure had gone. Everyone was cooperative, and no one thought to play the hero. Cash was appreciative almost to the point of thanking each of these good people for being so agreeable.

After Steve tied the cord securely around the bulging sack, he walked over to his partner, who could tell by the creases around Steve's eyes that he was grinning under the fabric of his kerchief. Cash noticed how Steve then took a minute to steadily eye each of the bank employees, as if determining what he should do with them. Cash could see that the sudden cold, venomous look in Reno's eyes had them scared. Hell, even Cash himself felt unsettled for an instant. But the robbery had gone off too perfectly for Steve to suddenly turn loco and start shooting up the place. Cash realized that he was simply giving a warning for the employees to stay put until the two of them were long gone.

Finally Steve started toward the door, and Cash back-stepped after him. Once outside, the pair hastily leaped upon their mounts and hightailed it out of town. When they were miles away and apparently free from pursuit, Steve could no longer hold the reins on his excitement and let loose with a series of high-pitched whoops. A relieved and overjoyed Cash quickly joined in.

They had pulled it off—with neither a shot fired nor a single word spoken.

And that should have been the end of the story. At least Cash McCall's part in it. Their first bank job was an unqualified success. As the partners counted out the money at the hideout Steve Reno had earlier chosen—a deserted little prospector's cabin miles away from Hensford and nestled deeply among the rocky foothills of Break Ridge Canyon—they found that they had almost twelve thousand dollars to split between them. The farmers had been especially generous with their deposits.

Cash was surprised, though, to see that Steve seemed a little disappointed. He explained his displeasure by saying he'd heard that it had been a good growing season and had expected their take to be even more. Closer to twenty or maybe thirty thousand.

Cash was satisfied with his end and remarked that it would see him well for a long time, but it was clear his partner didn't share his sense of gratitude. Or maybe he was just restless, eager to again experience that rush of excitement they'd both felt galloping out of town. If that was the case, Cash could readily understand his attitude. Hell, you couldn't get that giddy on a good drunk.

Spending long days cooped up in that godforsaken cabin— unable to venture into any of the small surrounding saloon towns to part with some of their bank proceeds, since it was still too soon for their trail to have cooled—began to gnaw at Steve. It didn't help that it seemed to rain constantly, the heavy pellets beating down on the roof of the cabin like a nonstop parade drumbeat. Worse from both their standpoints, they were running low on coffee and tobacco. Didn't have much vittles left, either, but that wasn't as much a concern, since neither Steve nor Cash was a big eater and could happily subsist on canned beans and biscuits. More important were their horses, both geldings. They had plenty of feed but were tied out back and forced to endure the relentless downpour.

Steve occupied his time by mapping out plans for another robbery, though not with any specific town or bank in mind. Cash hoped he was just relieving some of his boredom with his planning, since he knew they had been lucky in Hensford, and he, for one, didn't expect to have the same run of luck twice.

Steve had soon made it clear he wasn't so cautious. Sitting hunched over the small wood table, avoiding eye contact with his partner while he studied his pretend drawings, he said, "There ain't no difference with most of these farm banks."

"Might be now. After Hensford," Cash offered.

Steve wasn't listening. He went on. "We could walk into any one of 'em tomorrow and come out with another sackful of money."

Cash picked up a tiny, thin piece of wood and slid it between his lips as if it were a toothpick. "How d'you figure?"

Steve regarded him with amusement. " 'How'? 'Cause ain't no one dumb enough to take a bullet for some farmer's savings. Them yokels would rather stare down a gun from a horse thief."

"Reckon it depends on how serious the sheriff takes his job," Cash drawled, sucking on the sliver of wood.

"We can take our lesson from Hensford," Steve said. "Ain't seen no posse out ridin' after us."

"Yeah. But we ain't left this shack long enough to find out," Cash reminded him.

Steve pushed his chair away from the table and stood up. He began to pace. "Well, compadre, I can't sit around here no longer. Another coupla days listenin' to this damn rain, and I'll be chasin' mice."

"So why don't we just take what we got and ride outta here?" Cash suggested. "Set off south. Things have probably quieted some by now."

Steve nodded absently. "That's what we're gonna do. But I aim to be clearin' out a mite richer than I am."

"Thinkin' that's a mistake," Cash said.

"You wasn't so keen on Hensford, neither," Steve said slyly.

Finally Cash spoke the words that he knew Steve didn't want to hear. "We got lucky in Hensford."

Steve's eyes narrowed. "Wasn't no 'luck.' We just played the right percentages."

"Look at it any way you want. But count me out," Cash said flatly.

Steve focused his stare on his partner and took a long while before saying, "Can't do it alone."

But he couldn't change Cash's mind. His partner was dead set against it.

"I got what I came for," he said. "More, in fact. What good's a pocketful of spendin' money if you're dead or rotting in some jail cell?"

Steve finally relaxed his stare. He wore an odd smirk but didn't speak. He turned away from Cash and walked to the far side of the cabin, gazing out the small pane of glass that served as a window. It didn't provide much of a view, opening wet and blurry upon a surrounding border of large boulders and appendages of deadwood. Good protection maybe, but monotonous scenery.

He spoke without turning around. "Hate to lose a good partner, Cash. But if I gotta convince you, you'd be of no use to me."

"Wouldn't do you no good to try to convince me *or* persuade me," Cash replied.

Steve shrugged. "Then I guess this is where we part company. You do what you gotta, and I'll see my own way through."

Steve walked over to him and extended his hand in a friendly gesture. Cash accepted his handshake.

"No hard feelin's," Steve said.

"Glad to hear that. Wish you luck."

Steve grinned broadly. "Like I told you, don't put no value on luck."

Cash didn't ask Steve where he was planning to go. Frankly, he did not want to know. His partner had made his choice, and

Cash had made his, though Cash admittedly was sorry to see them part. After Steve stuffed his share of the bank money into his saddlebag and rode off through the rain that was still coming down, Cash knew that he would have to figure out his own next move. It was strange, but he and Steve had been partners for so long, he'd rarely made a decision solely on his own.

He would be safe inside the cabin, at least for a while, and so he decided to stay put until the rain stopped. The one good thing about all that rain coming down was that it would sure enough wash away their tracks.

But the rain didn't let up for two days, and by that time the posse from Hensford showed up and moved in on Cash late one night while he was asleep. Cash was exhausted and groggy when he awoke to a shuffling disturbance, and the whole event suddenly came upon him like a bad dream. Only when he felt the pain after he was roughly manhandled by the eager bunch did Cash fully understand that his capture was no nightmare. But what was soon about to happen most definitely was.

There was no point in trying to claim his innocence; Cash had carelessly left his share of the bank money strewn all over the table. One of the posse even sort of thanked him, saying that Cash had made it mighty easy for them.

Hensford was a small community populated by simple folks who had a basic way of looking at right and wrong: right was right, wrong was wrong. No middle area. They demanded justice at this outrage committed against their town, and they got it. Cash was surprised to find that they'd checked his background pretty thoroughly and discovered that he'd been freed on an earlier store robbery charge back in Wyoming. But what surprised him even more was when his mother appeared in the courtroom and tearfully told the judge and the spectators that her son was really a good boy who'd grown up fatherless and made a few wrong choices. Her intentions were well-meaning, but what Cash believed had decided it for the tough old judge was when Ma told the courtroom outright that she was having problems with her younger son, Ethan, and that his brother was the only one who could set him on the right path. Considering Cash's crime and the little "misjudgment" in his past, the judge obviously thought otherwise and promptly sentenced Cash McCall to six years in the Territorial Prison at Bennetsville.

As he was throughout most of the proceedings, Cash was numb after the judge passed sentence. All he would remember was his mother crying and the look of relief on his court-appointed lawyer's face that it was over.

Two years into his sentence Cash's old partner, Steve Reno, was apprehended. Cash was glad to see a familiar face, while at the same time he tried to avoid close contact with Steve, knowing that camaraderie with him presented the potential for trouble with the guards. Trouble that Cash sure wasn't looking for. But within the confines of prison, with its exclusive society, avoiding Reno proved difficult—especially since Steve seemed insistent and persistent about talking with him. Cash had to admit he was curious, and the two finally spoke when they were given a ten-minute afternoon rest period from their labor.

Cash had known Steve Reno since they were kids. What most impressed Cash about his friend was how Steve always presented himself well. He even managed to look good in his black-and-white-striped prison issue. He was well groomed, with his black hair neatly combed and glossy with tonic. Steve had personality to spare, which made him a fine companion and compensated for his somewhat sinister appearance. He wasn't what one would call handsome, exactly; rather, he had an odd, somewhat predatory look. Narrow-faced with a prominent bone structure, thin-lipped and possessing a strong arched nose. But what always stood out most about Steve Reno were his eyes. They were deep set and the coldest of blue. They were eyes that told you outright: *Don't ever cross me*. And if one was smart, one heeded their silent warning. Although he could display politeness and fine manners, he also possessed a hair-trigger temper that could see him switch from charm to rage in an instant—with or without provocation. But Steve rarely got his own hands dirty. He ran with a gang of toughs who were more than obliging when it came to stepping in for Steve and inflicting punishment on whomever Steve had a particular dislike for. Steve Reno had a lot of friends like that. So it came as little surprise that Steve—calling himself The Whiskey Kid to impress the inmates—soon became one of the most popular convicts in the prison, even among the veterans who were either suspicious of or openly hostile toward the "punks." He was even treated with a kind of respect by the guards. It didn't take Cash long to figure out that Steve's lenient treatment had to do with his forming some influential "friendships" during the two years that Cash himself had been locked away.

Because of his situation, Cash hadn't had the opportunity to make such friends. Not that it was ever his intention. Where Steve and he differed—and this distinction became much clearer to Cash during the many sleepless nights in his cell—was that Steve truly desired the life of an outlaw. Cash had gone along with him in Hensford only because he was young and restless and eager to make some quick, easy money. And, of course, Steve always knew just how to persuade him. But prison life had made a difference to Cash. Once he got his release from Bennetsville, he would be putting his guns aside forever.

Still, he had to admit, he liked Steve. His pleasant, easygoing nature appealed to him, though he was as aware as anyone else who knew Steve of the man's volatile moods, never knowing when some person or situation would strike the match to set off a charge of dynamite.

The ten-minute break period was the one opportunity when the rules granted the inmates the opportunity to speak to one another. Naturally no one was willing to say too much, since the guards hovered over the prisoners like vultures, always within earshot and eager for just the slightest infraction of the rules, such as whispered conversation.

Cash could still remember Steve's first words as he seated himself next to his former partner on a large rock.

"Well, compadre, reckon I didn't plan those percentages as well as I thought." There was no regret in his voice, only resignation.

Cash was a little taken aback. "You sayin' they got you for that job we pulled in Hensford?"

Steve grinned. When his mood was good, he always grinned, flashing the straightest set of teeth Cash had ever seen.

"Ain't that a hell of a thing? Stayed clean for a while, spent my money, and had a good time. Maybe *too* good. Yeah, after two years I hardly expected to be brought in on that one—and if I was, I woulda thought that maybe it was you who talked. But that ain't the case. Messed up myself. Got good and drunk one night and started shootin' my mouth off to this saloon girl. Reckon that woulda been all right . . . if'n I'd only paid her later."

Cash shook his head in wonderment. "And you was the one that said never trust no saloon wench."

Steve bent his arms stiffly at the elbow and stretched backward.

"You learn by your mistakes," he said, exhaling a deep breath. "But you can bet that's one I won't be repeatin'."

Before the guards ordered the men to resume the silence that preceded their return to work, Steve winked at Cash and said something that would stay with him.

"The way I got it figured, I'm gonna get myself a good education here."

And he did. After that meeting, Steve didn't come too close to his old partner, preferring the company of the lifers and other hard cases, into whose ranks he blended easily. He'd gotten off comparatively easy and had only a five-year term to serve, and he was determined to make every minute count.

The day before Cash was to be released, he saw Steve for what he thought would be the last time. During their years of imprisonment the two had never shared a meal together, but on Cash's final night in the supper hall, Steve chose to sit away from his usual group and come eat with him. He was grinning that contagious grin of his that stood out from the solemn faces of the other convicts crowded around their tables.

Since prisoners were forbidden to speak during meals, he placed a hand over his mouth and spoke in a low voice, keeping a wary eye out for passing guards.

"Congratulations, compadre. I hear that tomorrow you're in the graduatin' class."

Cash was still a trifle sore at what he saw as Steve's favored treatment by the inmates and, especially, many of the guards.

"Seems to me, whatever influence you got coulda made my last few years a mite more comfortable," he said, speaking through his fingers and in the same hushed tone.

"Yeah, well, my favors only go so far," Steve replied. "But I'm gonna make it up to you. Once I walk outta here."

Cash risked insulting Steve when he whispered back, "I won't be needin' that kind of 'favor.'"

Steve wasn't offended. "Don't be too quick, compadre," he simply said. "You can't never know for sure when you'll need a friend."

"I'll be fine," Cash said. He took a sip of the tar that masqueraded as coffee and added, with a bitter edge to his voice, "The one good thing that came outta this is, if I could survive six years in this hellhole, I can survive anything."

"Mebbe," Steve said with a slight, enigmatic smile. "But lemme tell you, when I walk outta here, it's gonna be a whole different story. Ain't gonna be playin' by nobody's rules 'cept my own."

And with those final words Cash felt that his association, and maybe his friendship, with Steve Reno was finished. Cash would be moving back to the town where they both were born and grew up, and Steve, as The Whiskey Kid, once he was released, would be going to wherever his lawless pursuits would take him. Cash, for one, was sure of that. His former partner had made a major step in his criminal ambitions. It was as clear as a blue-water pond that prison hadn't made him repentant, only more determined to succeed on the outside, and inadvertently had provided him with the right tools.

But as Cash considered, who was he to pass judgment? Maybe he wouldn't be following the same path as Steve Reno, but he definitely knew that he wouldn't be leaving prison with a more tolerant view of society.

Early the next morning a burly guard escorted Cash from his cell into the warden's office. The warden greeted him solemnly, wordlessly. Cash collected his belongings and the meager pay he had earned for almost working himself to death, feeling no obligation to thank the warden for these few dollars. After six years he finally changed from his prison uniform into the clothes he had worn when he first stepped through the prison gates. He'd lost a lot of weight, and his clothing hung off him like rags. He had to keep tugging at his belt to keep his pants up, but he didn't care. It was a minor inconvenience. He was finally a free man and about to be out of this stinking dungeon. A place Cash Mc-Call vowed he would never set foot in again. He'd sooner take a bullet between the eyes than ever again suffer the tortures of the Territorial Prison at Bennetsville.

A wagon was outside the gates, waiting to take Cash and some of the other newly liberated prisoners the several miles to the stage-coach station. From there would come a long ride to the railroad depot and train transportation, then another long stage ride to Wyatt City, the Wyoming town where Cash was born and his mother and younger brother still called home.

By the time Cash climbed aboard the train, he was bone-tired from the dusty journey. But try as he might, he couldn't get any shut-eye. Even the gentle rhythm of motion and the *clackety-clack* of the wheels rolling along the expanse of track couldn't relax him. He had too many things running through his head. He was going home, and he wasn't sure if he was ready to deal with that. He knew his ma would be glad to see him, as would his brother, Ethan—and *that* was one of the reasons for his uncertainty.

He remembered how Ma had said in the courtroom that Ethan was starting to get himself into trouble. He'd always been a bit on the wild side, almost from the time he could walk, and, with no man around to control him, Cash could well imagine the problems their mother might be having.

Ethan was nineteen now, and if he hadn't settled his behavior some in the years that his brother had been away from home, he was well on his way to serving his own time in prison.

Cash felt kind of responsible. When Ethan most needed a man around, Cash was off running with Steve Reno—and later paying with six years of his life for the wisdom of that association.

Ethan never knew the old man. But Cash remembered him—and that wasn't saying a lot. He was never around much, preferring the atmosphere and male companionship of saloons—not to mention the comforts provided by the saloon girls. Cash recalled that his father's biggest problem was that he liked to gamble but wasn't very good at it. He'd put down money on any card game and usually lose his whole week's pay in a single sitting. After trying to console himself with a few stiff belts of whiskey, he'd stagger home and take out his frustrations on his wife. It wasn't exactly a sad day when the old man just up and left and never came back.

Of course that meant that Ma had to go to work, since she still had two boys to look after. She did some waitressing, took in laundry, and even did chores for the neighbors. She worked herself to the bone each and every day just so her sons could have a roof over their heads and sufficient grub to eat. She always seemed to be working, and all she asked of Cash was to keep an eye on his brother.

But Cash had inherited a lot of his old man's personality. He plainly wasn't interested in responsibility, school, or any form of discipline. He hardly saw the inside of a classroom and started farming Ethan out to neighbors while he took to roaming the streets with Steve Reno and their other shantytown pals.

Then Ethan grew older and wanted to join in on his brother's wayward path. He was regularly truant from school, and who was Cash to tell him otherwise? It wasn't long before Ma found out, and Cash got the lecture about responsibility and being the "man of the house." But he wasn't having any of it. The way he saw it, he was helping to support the family, suckering Ma into believing that he was holding down a variety of odd jobs while he was really throwing cash onto the table that he'd earned through petty thievery and back-alley gambling.

Of course Steve Reno was always around, and Ethan looked up to him with almost the same respect he had for his older brother. Even at a young age Steve had a bravado about him that captivated the kid, and he filled Ethan's head with stories about how one day he and Cash would be running the town and calling the shots. That's where Cash finally drew the line. He still had enough sense about him to not encourage the kid's already wild imagination.

Cash thought regretfully that he would have been wise to heed his own advice.

Once his train pulled into Wyoming, Cash walked into town and deposited his belongings at the stagecoach station. Since he would have to wait a few hours for the next stage to ride through, he checked his money and decided to wander into the general store to pick out some little trinket for Ma. She knew he was coming home, but he still wanted to surprise her with a better gift than just himself. Yet he felt miserable as he paid a couple of dollars for a pair of cheap earrings. He remembered the loot he'd gotten from the Hensford bank job and thought about what he could have done for Ma with that kind of cash. He deliberately neglected to remind himself that sharing his ill-gotten gains with his family had been the furthest thing from his mind at the time.

It was early evening of the next day when the stage rumbled onto the road leading to Wyatt City. As it crossed east through western Wyoming that morning, Cash breathed in the clean, fresh air through the open window of the stage, though it troubled him that he was still unable to rid his nostrils of the stench from Bennetsville. While he'd enjoyed admiring and absorbing the scenery of his home state, particularly the mountain ranges and rangelands of the Rocky Mountains West—especially impressive under the wide, clear country skies—Cash was relieved when the journey was finally over.

He was plumb tuckered out. Before heading home he decided to visit one of his old haunts, a saloon called Dead Eye Molly's, and have a drink and relax for a spell. Cash moseyed in through the swinging batwings and noted that the place was just as dark, dingy, and smelly as he remembered it. Still, it was the first familiar thing he'd seen in six years, and he needed a small taste of familiarity before being faced with the reality of being home. There were only a few sad-looking drunks scattered about the saloon, each drowning his own misery in cheap whiskey. Cash paid them no mind and went up to the bar.

An old crone named Molly Ferguson was the owner of this "palace." She was a really unattractive woman who justly came by her nickname because one of her eyes—her right eye—had a milky blue-gray cast, and the orb itself never moved.

Dead Eye Molly's was actually a front for Molly's more lucrative sideline as the procurer and seller of stolen merchandise. Cash doubted her saloon ever made a profit, since it was a backstreet establishment whose only patrons were the types proper folks would never want to keep company with. Molly was always handing out free shots or putting drinks on credit for luckless customers who she knew would never settle their accounts. But Molly's side business more than compensated for her saloon losses. Ugly as she was, Molly was shrewd—and altogether ruthless when it came to running the affairs of her other enterprise. She had established a list of contacts throughout the territory to whom she could unload stolen goods for handsome profits. It worked well for her, since most of her customers were amateur thieves eager to pawn their ill-gotten merchandise for quick cash. Molly knew she had the upper hand in these negotiations and paid pennies on the dollar, while she built herself a tidy bankroll.

When the bartender came up to the other side of the counter and asked what Cash wanted, Cash didn't know what the hell to ask for. It had been a long time since he'd last tasted alcohol. So he just blurted, "Gimme somethin' strong."

He didn't know why, but he next asked, "Is Molly around?"

The bartender grunted, poured Cash a shot of whiskey, and walked to the other end of the bar, disappearing down the corridor toward a back room. Cash didn't know the guy but noted that he was short and stocky and almost as ugly as Molly.

Cash downed his drink quickly and a few moments later turned his head when he saw Molly hobble out of the back room, followed by her bartender. She was wearing what almost looked like a sackcloth with a filthy apron tied around her waist. Cash could tell right away that Molly had gotten a lot older and heavier. And that sure did nothing to improve her looks. She'd also taken to wearing a patch over her affected eye. Cash had to give her credit for one thing, though. She was a gargoyle, and she knew it, even going so far as to name her saloon after her deformity.

She went behind the bar and came over to Cash, gazing at him curiously out of her one good eye. Cash instantly regretted asking for her.

As she got closer, a cigarette drooping from her lips, she suddenly stopped as an expression of recognition crossed her unpleasant features.

"Well, well, Cash McCall," she said, her voice near a hoarse whisper from tobacco and drinking the rotgut she served. Then she broke into a coughing spasm, finally spitting up whatever was lodged in her throat onto the floor.

"Howdy, Molly," Cash said in as pleasant a voice as he could manage.

He didn't expect to hear what she next told him. "Your brother's been around."

Cash could feel the anger begin to surge. This was not news he wanted to hear his first minutes back in town. He quickly realized he had to harness his temper.

Molly wore an expression that suggested she knew that Cash was ready to crawl all over her for saying what she had, and she feebly tried to soothe him.

"He's a good kid, McCall. Jus' like you."

"Who's he been comin' in here with?" Cash asked.

"Jus' some of the other boys. They're nice kids too," Molly said slyly.

"Yeah," Cash said abruptly.

Wisely, Molly changed the subject. "You jus' get out?"

Cash nodded curtly and asked Molly for some tobacco and a paper for a cigarette. Instead she pulled out a silver cigarette case from the flap in her apron and handed him a ready-made smoke. She watched quietly as he took a match from those stuffed inside a shot glass on the bar and lit it.

"Reckon ya saw The Kid," she said, referring to Steve Reno.

"I saw him."

"He's another good boy," Molly remarked with another sly grin.

Cash had had enough. Coming in here had been a mistake. His head swimming from the liquor he'd been away from for six years, he tossed Molly a mean look, slapped some silver down onto the bar, and strode outside to where the air was a lot cleaner.

He felt all coiled up inside, like a rattler getting ready to strike. He knew he couldn't let Ma see him like that and hoped a walk might clear the alcohol from his brain and cool him down. He walked aimlessly for quite a spell, and when he finally came to the little house at the edge of town, the skies were getting dark, smudged with purplish clouds. A sliver of moon was just visible among the faint sparkling of the stars. Cash couldn't recall any of the routes he'd taken, since he was still trying to put some order to the thoughts that were spinning around in his brain.

There was a table lamp lit inside the house, casting a muted yellow glow outside through the curtainless window in the parlor, a welcoming beacon for the wayward son. Cash stood outside the gate for a while before he finally entered the small yard and approached the front door. It was strange, but those few moments seemed almost as long to him as his six-year prison sentence.

Finally he knocked. After all this time Cash didn't think it right that he should just walk in.

Ma answered the door. When she saw that it was her son standing there, she at first appeared very calm. Cash was a bit surprised by her reaction but not disappointed. He didn't know if he could handle any show of emotion.

Yet the closer he looked at her in those quick seconds of a silence that he found mighty awkward, Cash could see the glimmer of tears in her eyes.

"Hello, Ma," he finally said.

She started to say something but then stopped herself and instead threw her arms around his waist and pressed her head against his chest.

Cash felt uncomfortable and just wanted to pull away. But he let her have her moment; then he gently began maneuvering her inside the house.

He looked around the parlor and into the kitchen. Nothing had changed.

Ma had followed and was now standing in front of him, giving him a critical look.

"You've gotten so thin, Cashton," she said with a typical mother's concern. "You haven't been eating."

Cash just gave her a smile.

"Well, you've got to eat," she said firmly. "You must be hungry."

"Yeah, I am," he said, trying to sound enthused, though his years of digesting prison grub had pretty much soured him on food. "Ain't had anythin' close to a decent meal in a long time."

"Supper will be ready soon. I made your favorite: chicken and corn bread. And peach pie for dessert. Why don't you go sit yourself, and I'll pour you a nice cup of coffee."

What Cash really could have used was another shot of whiskey. But since the old man left, Ma didn't keep liquor around the house.

Ma ushered him over to the armchair that had seen better days. Before Cash sat, he glanced into the dark bedroom that he and his brother had shared.

"Where's Ethan?" he asked.

Ma seemed uneasy. "Oh, he just went out for a little walk. He'll be back soon."

Cash nodded, though he sensed Ma could tell he didn't believe her.

"How long's he been gone?"

Ma was quick to reply. "Not long. I'm sure he'll back in time for supper. He knows you were coming home today."

Ma started for the kitchen. Cash said softly, "You're gonna have to be tellin' me 'bout him."

Ma turned back to him and rocked her head. "I know," she said, her voice sounding strained. "But not now. Tonight's your night, and I don't want anything to spoil it."

Cash didn't want to upset his mother and so let the matter drop—for now—and instead settled his tired body back into the armchair in the corner.

The upshot was that his brother, Ethan, apparently so eager to see Cash, never came home for supper. Cash ate a very quiet meal with Ma. Rather, Cash ate. He noticed with some concern that his mother just picked at the small portions on her plate.

Ethan still hadn't come home by the time Cash went to bed, which was just before eleven thirty. Ma had retired earlier, and Cash had sat up reading for a spell, waiting for his brother's return before finally giving in to his exhaustion. At about four in the morning some sort of gut feeling snapped him awake just before he heard the slow creak of the front door opening. Cash listened carefully as someone crept into the house. Then the door to the bedroom opened, and Cash saw the silhouette of Ethan standing on the threshold.

It was too dark in the room for Ethan to know Cash was there. He couldn't see that his brother was awake and quietly watching him.

Cash waited until Ethan flopped into bed, still fully clothed, and then his voice cut through the blackness.

"Where you been, kid?"

"Cash, is that you?" Ethan's voice blended both excitement and a hint of uncertainty.

Cash reached over and lit the bedside lantern. When the glow was sufficient, he saw that Ethan was on his side facing him, propped up on an elbow, his expression shadowed.

Cash was still only half-awake and realized that it probably wasn't the best time to say anything. But he did have some words that needed speaking. He kept his voice low, so as not to waken Ma. But what he said could hardly be mistaken for a pleasant greeting.

"Don't matter to me that you wasn't home tonight. But it meant somethin' to Ma, your bein' here."

"Look, Cash, can't we . . . can't we talk 'bout this in the mornin'?"

Cash curtly ignored his suggestion. "You been doin' this for the last six years?" he wanted to know.

"Doin' what?" Now the kid sounded annoyed.

"Not comin' home."

"I'm home lotsa the time." Ethan screwed up his face into a puzzled expression. "What're you gettin' at anyway?"

"Are you really that dumb, kid?"

Cash pulled the sheets off and twisted himself into a sitting position at the side of the bed. He fixed his eyes squarely on the kid, getting his first good look at him.

He wasn't prepared for what he saw and guessed that the shock must have registered on his face. He really couldn't be sure of how long it had been since he'd last seen his brother, but it was obvious he wasn't looking at a kid anymore. Physically, at least, Ethan had grown into a mature, attractive man. Hell, Cash thought, his looks alone could guarantee him a fine life. It would be nice to say that, as his brother, Ethan shared Cash's looks, but Cash would have been flattering himself. The only thing they seemed to have in common was a punk attitude.

Cash suddenly felt ashamed and embarrassed, thinking of the lost years between them. For the moment he couldn't speak what was on his mind.

His obvious hesitation gave Ethan the chance to change the subject. "Was it tough, Cash?" he asked quietly. "Prison, I mean."

Cash managed to find firmness in his voice when he answered, "Kid, I'm gonna make it so you never find out."

Chapter Two

Cash didn't fool himself for an instant that he was going to have an easy time trying to straighten out his brother. From what he remembered, Ethan could be like an unbridled stallion, determined to chase down his own path. Something Cash recognized from his own restless youth.

From the moment Cash stepped off the stage in Wyatt City, he'd wondered what the reception would be in his hometown. Everyone knew who he was—and what he'd gone to prison for. It sure wasn't the celebrity he wanted. But what he found most disturbing was how he was looked up to by Ethan and, especially, by his brother's friends. Cash McCall had gained a notoriety that, it soon became apparent, some of those kids wanted to emulate. Most of Ethan's "playmates" came from the poor part of town and admired Cash because he'd shown no respect for the rules that kept them and their families mired in poverty. They saw crime as the only way to escape the bleakness of their lives. And Cash had provided an example.

Cash could be sympathetic to their situation. But he had no desire to encourage their criminal ambitions.

Setting Ethan on the right track was only one of his problems. If he was going to set any kind of *good* example, he was going to have to find himself a job. That wouldn't be easy, since he was the first to admit he'd never worked an honest day in his life. If he was lucky enough to find anything, Cash knew it would only be slightly better than the labor he'd been forced to do in prison.

And he would have to be grateful even for that, thanks to the brand of his reputation.

Cash was up early the next morning. Ethan was still asleep, so he had a light breakfast of toast and coffee with Ma. He finished up with a piece of leftover pie. There was only a quarter of the dessert left in the pan. Ethan had evidently gotten up during the night and helped himself to a generous slice. Cash was a light sleeper, but even he had not heard him leave the room. He now figured out how Ethan had been managing to sneak out of the house at night without Ma knowing. Cash had to say this much: the kid could move like a cat. He had the makings of a good burglar.

While they sat at the table, Ma still seemed reluctant to tell Cash about the problems she was having with Ethan. Cash finally had to remind her that he was home now and would help in any way he could.

"But it ain't gonna be easy, Ma," he said with a deep sigh. "Six years is a long time."

"Cashton . . . it—it was hard enough seeing you go away," Ma said. "I don't know what I'd do if Ethan . . ." Her words and voice trailed off, and she lowered her head.

"Turned out like me?" Cash finished for her, his words betraying some self-pity.

Ma was quick to reply. "No," she said adamantly. "You did wrong. But you paid for your mistake, and it's behind you now. There's no reason you can't make a clean start."

Cash gave an empty nod but didn't voice what he was thinking: *Sure. A clean start. If the citizens will let me.*

Cash reached across the table and gently took both of Ma's hands in his own. Her hands were old and slightly arthritic, tracked with veins. As he studied her troubled features, he noticed how much she'd aged in the six years that he'd been gone. She hadn't gotten older—just old. A telling sign of the difficult life she had lived. She was only in her early fifties, but she looked worn and tired. Her once carefully styled full head of auburn hair had turned a dull gray and was thinning, and she no longer let it hang loose proudly over her shoulders but had it pulled back and tied with a ribbon. Cash had to admit that he almost could not recognize her now. Ma had always worked hard and without complaint for him and Ethan, and Cash was consumed with a deep shame that he hadn't done much—hell, he hadn't done *anything*—to repay her.

He could tell Ma had more to say, something that she seemed to be struggling against telling him. He gently urged her to continue.

Ma tilted the coffee cup to her lips, hesitated, then placed it back on the saucer.

She spoke haltingly. "Cashton . . . I haven't been well. I didn't want to say anything while you were away because I didn't want you to worry. But . . . I haven't been able to keep working."

Her words were like a quick punch to the jaw. Cash had a suspicion of what it really was that she didn't want to tell him. Something he'd suspected but made himself not think about while serving time at Bennetsville. Ma had been forced to go on charity. His "welcome home" meal had been provided by the generosity of neighbors.

"It's okay, Ma," Cash said, trying to keep his voice steady against the rush of blood churning in his head.

It took some prodding from Cash to learn that over the past several months Ma had begun to suffer severe headaches and dizzy spells. She assured Cash that the town doctor, Doc Pedersen, had told her that her condition was nothing serious and that she just needed to rest more. Cash wasn't convinced. Ma never would have quit working unless whatever was wrong with her *was* serious. But she kept insisting that she was all right and that neither Ethan nor he should worry, and Cash knew Ma was just as mule-headed stubborn as her boys, and it wouldn't do any good to argue with her.

"I'm home now, Ma, and I'm gonna make things better," he told her.

It was a promise Cash had known he would have to make her. Now he only had to find some way to keep it.

Gradually Cash learned about the trouble Ethan had been getting into. Minor stuff for the most part, but from Ma's words and things he recognized from his own past, he could see that his brother was aiming for bigger goals.

To appease his mother, Ethan had held down a few jobs—menial work like cleaning out stalls at the livery stable—but he was giving in more frequently to the same restlessness that Cash had gone through at his age. A job at the mercantile ended abruptly when he was caught stealing, and only Ma's pleadings to the store owner had saved Ethan from being carted off to jail. Because of episodes like that, he now was unable to find any kind of work in town—not even shoveling horse manure.

What was worse, he didn't seem to care.

"I'm makin' money," he said to Cash, taking a typical defiant stance. "But I ain't earnin' it by doin' what they say I should."

"How's that?"

Ethan gestured wildly—the stallion broken free. "Cheatin' me on my time ledger to short me on my pay. Workin' five hours and only gettin' paid for four 'cause they say I wasn't doin' my job. Yeah, and when they'd short me on my pay, I'd just take what they owed me—from their stock. But that ain't the way it's gonna be for me no longer. If no one else has to put it square on the barrel, why should I?"

Cash let his brother know that his arguments didn't impress him, even though it was like he was listening to himself ten years ago. Cash's own arguments likewise made little impression on Ethan, because he wasn't having any luck finding a job with his prison past and limited skills, and when Cash cornered him, Ethan countered by reminding his brother that *he* had finally decided just to take what he wanted.

The main difference between the brothers was that Ethan thought he was tough. Cash *was* tough. He didn't go around trying to prove it with a reckless bravado, looking for fights with bigger guys who could easily knock him into tomorrow. But his time spent at Bennetsville had hardened Cash beyond what he was before he entered the place. He'd seen and gone through too much *not* to be changed by the experience. He saw men lose their minds, carted off in screaming fits to the "dungeons," where God knows what became of them. Almost daily he witnessed men lose their souls to the brutality of the guards. Then there were those who were so broken by the whole experience, they simply cheated the state and took their own lives.

Those who succeeded were the lucky ones. The few who failed in their attempts were barely nursed back to health before enduring a long confinement in the hellfire pit known as "the hole."

So Cash knew the destination of the path Ethan was riding on, and nothing his brother could say would convince Cash to take his side. Brother or not, to Cash he was just a punk with a lot to learn.

But Ethan was wise to the difficult time Cash was having trying to get a job. His criminal past had made him popular with Ethan's street friends and maybe some of the town's other "less desirables," but it did nothing to impress an honest employer.

Still, Cash made the rounds every day, even borrowing a horse to ride out into the surrounding territory to see if he might get work as a ranch hand or ride along on a spring cattle drive, but each day ended on a note of disappointment. There simply were no jobs—at least not for Cash McCall. And Ethan would always be at home waiting for his brother to return, wearing a knowing smirk that Cash had to hold himself back from knocking off his face. Yeah, Cash thought resentfully, he was setting a fine example for the kid. The best he could do was not let his discouragement show. Ma helped with that by trying to maintain a cheery and optimistic outlook, as she had during those tough years when her boys were growing up. But just as Cash had as a kid, he could see through the transparency of her smile and knew that despite her "tomorrow will be a better day" facade, her true attitude was becoming just as defeated as his own.

The truth was, Cash hated his situation, and he detested not being honest with himself. He didn't want to be home. He resented that Ma was living off friendly charity while her two boys couldn't—or, in Ethan's case, *wouldn't*—find work. More than all that, he resented being saddled with the responsibility of watching over his brother. His being home seemed to make no real change in Ethan, even after Cash was finally forced to throw a punch at him to keep him respectful to Ma.

Cash only had to hit Ethan the one time and was careful to keep the reins on his temper. He hit him a gut shot because he didn't want to chance messing up his face. Everything else might have been rotten with the kid, but he'd been blessed with handsome

features that Ma was proud of, and she would never have for-
given Cash if he'd ruined them.

But Cash was angry. And he grew more bitter every day.

If Cash McCall was honest with himself, he would admit that he
had plenty of vices, from gambling to stealing to women. But hard
drinking had never been one of them. He used liquor more as a
way to calm his nerves. And after only a couple of weeks at home,
feeling nearly as confined as he had in his small prison cell, he decided that his nerves definitely needed some calming.

He hadn't been to Dead Eye Molly's since that first day he'd
come back into town. It wasn't where he really wanted to go, but
it was nearby, and a walk in the night air would do him good.

The streets were slick and the main road muddy after a late-
afternoon rain, but the Wyoming air smelled as fresh after a downpour as Cash remembered it from long-ago years, and he almost
started to feel like his old self again. He briefly considered not going to the saloon. But he was almost there, and so he kept walking
in that direction.

That turned out to be a mistake.

He strolled inside and looked around. At first it looked as if
there were no customers, which was fine with him. He preferred
to drink alone and quietly.

Then, as he went over to the bar and ordered himself a shot, he
happened to glance over his shoulder to the back of the room.

The last guy in the world he wanted to see was seated by himself, off in a dark corner.

Slug Fletcher had a reputation so feared that even the tougher
punks in town kept a respectful distance. He was a brutal specimen
with a scarred, pushed-in face. A man who craved violence the way
many of Molly's low-life customers craved alcohol. The man ex-
uded pure menace, even in the aggressive way he moved, thrusting
his upper body forward like a bull getting ready to charge.

Slug had been a bare-knuckle fighter whose immense power
had damaged a lot of his opponents. It wasn't long before he killed
a man in the ring and was asked to "retire" from the sport. Afterward, he worked as a lookout in some of the saloons in Cheyenne

and Laramie. Gambling-house proprietors also considered Slug a useful addition, as he made an intimidating presence and always made sure gambling losses were paid up promptly, often by enforcing his own unique methods of persuasion.

Cash wondered if Slug had proven himself too effective in his work, as he was surprised to see him back in Wyatt City looking like a trail hand, unshaven and dressed in dirty buckskins.

Cash knew Slug better than he wanted to. He was a friend of Steve Reno and one of Steve's most valuable assets when it came to settling disputes.

Cash nearly broke out in a sweat when he saw Slug, looking as intimidating as ever. Slug spotted Cash instantly, glancing up from the plate of greasy slop that Molly served as digestible food. Cash gave a cordial nod and hoped that was that.

He was wrong.

Even with his back turned, Cash could sense that Slug was watching him, and he was starting to feel real uneasy. The place was so quiet Cash could hear Slug chomping and slurping on his supper. The bartender was standing across from Cash on the other side of the counter, and Cash noticed him acknowledge with a nod of his head some gesture from Slug. His eyes then settled on Cash before he flickered them in the direction of Slug's table.

"He wants to see you," the bartender said gruffly.

Cash hesitated a moment before he responded with the weakest nod. He gulped down his shot of whiskey and asked for another. He quickly corrected himself. "No, just leave the bottle."

Cash carried the whiskey and shot glass over to Slug's table and noticed how Slug watched him approach with a blank, lifeless expression.

If Steve Reno had eyes that could suggest threat, Slug Fletcher's eyes just made you want to look away. They were cold, black, and grim, set under fierce eyebrows, and hinted of murderous intent. They mirrored the soul of a man who had no qualms about committing violence. A man who, if he had to inflict pain first . . . well, that was considered a bonus.

"Howdy, Slug," Cash drew up the nerve to say.

Slug didn't return the greeting. He didn't even invite Cash to sit down. Instead he pulled a fat cigar from his breast pocket and lit it.

Cash took it upon himself to take a seat across from him and watched as he puffed on his cigar, blowing out smoke from the side of his mouth.

It seemed a long while before Slug finally said something.

Despite his gorilla girth and arms that could crush a man's spine into powder, Slug had a thin, raspy voice, the result, it was suspected, of having been punched once too often in his throat during his bare-knuckle fighting days.

Still, what he told Cash hit with the impact of a blow from one of his fists.

"Got a telegram coupla days ago. The Kid'll be out in a few weeks. Whaddya know 'bout that?"

Cash didn't want to express any look of surprise. You just didn't do that in front of Slug Fletcher. But he was stunned by the news. Steve Reno still had a solid year to go on his sentence, and Cash fully understood that the state was not quick to hand out early releases to any of the inmates at Bennetsville.

"I don't know nothin' 'bout it, Slug," Cash replied.

Slug eyed him suspiciously, the heavy smoke from his cigar now billowing about his face. Cash could tell he didn't trust his ignorance of the matter.

And then a thin, chilling smile crept across Slug's thick, wet lips. Cash barely managed to hold back a shudder. It was always unsettling to see a cold-blooded killer smile.

"All right, then," was all he said.

Cash hadn't even poured himself a shot from the bottle but was grateful that their little talk seemed to be over. He got up from the table.

"But don't be leavin' town," Slug said—and this wasn't a request. He was *telling* him. "The Kid says he wants to see ya when he gets out."

"He's—he's comin' back to Wyatt City?" Cash muttered.

Slug looked at him with that grim stare. "He was askin' 'bout how your brother's doin'," he added, and he left it at that.

Cash nodded. Their talk was finished, and he was relieved,

though puzzled and not a little concerned why Steve had asked about Ethan.

Slug continued to puff on his cigar. Cash could feel his eyes still on him as he turned from the table and tried to keep his gait steady as he went up to the counter to pay for his drink.

"Don't worry 'bout it," the bartender said. "It's been taken care of."

Chapter Three

Cash could not deny he was curious about Steve's wanting to see him when he got out of Bennetsville. He certainly had been surprised to learn that Steve was getting his release before serving his full sentence, and he had to wonder just who it was that was making the arrangements. Steve did have to have some mighty important and influential friends on the outside, judging by the way he was treated behind those high walls, but just who these friends were and how they had enough influence to fix things with the state's prison system had Cash bewildered.

Cash mulled this over until he came to the conclusion that whoever was working this out for Steve had to be someone inside the prison. Someone connected to the right people who could then fix all the necessary details. The Territorial Prison at Bennetsville was run strictly, with severe discipline the daily routine, but there had to be some corruption going on if a small-time desperado like Steve Reno could reap all those benefits he enjoyed while Cash and the other inmates were treated worse than pigs—and now get himself a pass before his time was served.

One thing was for certain, as Cash saw it. All this added up to Steve Reno's finally becoming the big man he sought to be: the Whiskey Kid of the history books. Whoever was "sponsoring" his release had to be pretty powerful—and likely had some powerful plans in mind for Steve.

Cash himself was somehow to fit into those plans; that much was made evident through Slug Fletcher. It wasn't a prospect that sat comfortably with him. He thought he'd seen the last of Steve after he walked through those prison gates. He fully intended to stick by his promise never to see the inside of a cell again. Having any dealings with Steve Reno was a sure guarantee to get him back there.

But now Slug Fletcher seemed to be back in the picture as well. The one guy nobody with an ounce of sense dared run afoul of. Cash didn't know how much sense he had, but he knew that, with Slug's involvement, he'd have to see Steve when he called.

There wasn't a damn thing he could do about it.

The week had ended on a miserable note, and the following Monday continued the trend. Cash had hardly slept a wink since meeting with Slug at the saloon Saturday night. His thoughts had become his own worst enemy—a problem he'd developed all those sleepless nights in prison. As he laid awake in the comfort of his own bed, he would become so troubled with all he was dealing with that his heart would start to pound and get heavy with pressure, as if his chest was being stepped on by an angry mule. The only way he could ease this tension was by surrendering to his discomfort and even accepting that dying wouldn't necessarily be the worst thing that could happen to him. Cash knew that he was too tough and stubborn to accept such a simple solution. But not fearing death and maybe even welcoming it for the release it would bring to the mess he'd made of his life somehow settled his distress.

One of his concerns was Ma's failing health. He could see how she seemed to be getting sicker in just the few weeks that he had been home. Cash had a dumb hope that maybe it was just his knowing she was sick that made her symptoms seem worse. But that couldn't explain the sight of her barely able to digest her food or the more frequent lay-downs she had to take during the day.

Although hard for Cash to admit, in a way he resented her. He couldn't help thinking that she'd waited until he got home before letting her sickness get the better of her. He felt that she knew she wasn't strong enough to go on worrying about Ethan and was now passing that burden on to him. What added to this frustration was that she still wouldn't admit to there being anything seriously wrong with her. Cash finally had to pay his own visit to Doc Pedersen to get the lowdown, and the doc confirmed that his mother was a lot sicker than she was letting on. He further told Cash that he'd written prescriptions for her but was informed by the druggist that she'd never had them filled. Cash guessed the reason was that Ma simply hadn't the money to afford medicines.

Cash recognized and acknowledged his own blame, the guilt that had gnawed away at his innards for six years. But he didn't know what Ethan would feel once he knew the truth about their mother. It hadn't taken Cash long to discover that the relationship Ethan had with Ma was one of little respect. He treated her more like a caring older sister than a mother, responding to her occasional scoldings with either a smirk or a false promise to behave himself. Like all liars, he could be convincing at that. Ethan's attitude toward his brother wasn't much better. They were cordial enough to each other, but their talks were brief and usually limited to Cash's questioning him about where he'd been or what he was up to. Ethan would give some offhand answer that Cash suspected wasn't the truth and then walk away and do what he wanted.

But for Ma's sake Cash wouldn't give up. He knew he couldn't tie the kid to his bed, much as he often would have liked, but he finally enforced a stern rule about Ethan's being home at a certain hour every night. His persuasion was that, if Ethan didn't follow these rules, Cash would lead him out back, where he'd teach him obedience in a way that he could readily understand. And it was getting so that Cash started not to care if he landed one on his brother's pretty face.

On Tuesday night Ethan was in another of his restless and downright cantankerous moods. He grumbled that he wanted to get out for some air and maybe stop at the mercantile for a sarsaparilla. Cash was reluctant to give him permission, since it was only about an hour till his curfew, but Ma was already in bed, and, frankly, Cash wasn't up to having the kid moping around the house. He told Ethan to be back in an hour, Ethan promised he would, and Cash settled back to read the newspaper and have a little time to himself. Around eight o'clock he started to get a real uneasy feeling that finally got him up from his armchair and out the door to check on his brother.

Cash strolled through town to the mercantile, where Ethan had said he'd be going. But when he checked with the clerk who was getting ready to close up shop, he was told that not only had Ethan not come in tonight, but the clerk hadn't seen him around for nearly a week.

That didn't surprise Cash a whole lot. In fact, he'd expected it, which was why his gut had told him to go out after his brother. Ethan was following the same path Cash had traveled at his age. He knew it too. Only he was too dumb to recognize the consequences.

Cash purchased some tobacco and papers from the clerk and started for the most likely place Ethan would be: the local pool hall.

The moment he turned onto Taylor Street, he saw the commotion.

The activity seemed to be focused on the alley that ran adjacent to the pool hall. Cash kept back as he watched the sheriff and two of his deputies emerge from the alley, flanking four young punks, two of whom they were leading out in manacles.

In an instant Cash recognized one of the kids as his brother.

Once they were out on the street, Cash moved impulsively toward Ethan. Their eyes locked, and in that moment of silence between them Cash couldn't restrain himself any longer.

"Punk!" he spat—and then he struck Ethan hard across the face. One of the deputies quickly grabbed Cash by the shoulders and pulled him back.

"McCall," the man said in warning, "go gittin' heavy-handed ag'in, and you'll be sharin' a cell with your brother."

Cash pulled away from his grip and glared at the deputy without a word.

Ethan was dazed—likely more shocked that his brother gave it to him in the face—but he swiftly recovered. Cash didn't feel the least bit of regret for hitting him. Not even knowing how it would have upset their mother. Ethan would have gotten a lot more if the deputy hadn't interfered.

Cash glanced out at the small crowd of spectators who had gathered around. One girl looked particularly troubled. She was a tiny thing, sweet-faced, with long chestnut-colored hair tied back in a ribbon. Cash noticed how she and Ethan looked directly at each other with expressions that told him this girl was familiar with Ethan and not just another casual bystander.

She had big expressive eyes, but her complexion was ghostly pale, made more so by the glow of the gaslit street lamp she stood under.

Then, as the lawmen hustled Ethan and his pals down the boardwalk toward the jail, the girl suddenly rushed over, only to be kept back by the sheriff. She was crying, but when she looked toward Cash, her pretty face twisted into a scowl. She couldn't have known that he was Ethan's brother, but it was apparent she didn't much appreciate Cash's hitting him.

Cash stared at her in silence, his expression betraying no emotion. He then moved toward the mouth of the alley and peered through the dark to a dim light provided by a lamp sitting on the ground against the outer wall of the pool hall. The town doctor was kneeling beside a man who was stretched out on his back and not moving.

Cash's heart started to race. When he turned his attention back to the street, the girl had disappeared. Cash had hoped to talk to her, find out if she knew what had happened. Instead he stood back and listened to the excited conversation among the bystanders.

What Cash heard was what he dreaded. His brother and his pals had jumped the man, who had won some tableside bets shooting billiards. But from what was being said, the guy apparently had put up such a fight that it gave a witness time to go for the sheriff.

Cash didn't know what, exactly, had been Ethan's part in this. But it was enough for him to know that his brother somehow had been involved and was arrested. There would be a trial, and in all likelihood the outcome would be grim.

As if I need to deal with this, Cash thought miserably to himself. But of course that was the kind of selfish attitude he would expect from his brother. The real concern was with Ma finding out. As Cash walked the now-quiet streets back home, building a cigarette, he struggled with how—and what—he was going to tell her. With her health being so poor, he was fearful of what learning this might do to her.

He decided it best not to say anything to her till morning. He couldn't disturb her needed rest with such terrible news. But he did expect a visit from the sheriff and so waited up in the parlor for his arrival. He would hear him coming up the porch and could get to the door before his knock wakened Ma.

If he didn't know it before, he sure knew now. He was in charge.

The sheriff came within the hour. Cash heard heavy footfalls start up the porch, and he hurried to the door. He undid the latch just as the sheriff was about to deliver a resounding knock. Cash opened the door and stepped outside, making it clear that he wouldn't be inviting the lawman inside.

"Howdy, McCall," the sheriff said.

The sheriff was Garrett O'Dowd, a kid Cash had grown up with. They had ended up on opposite sides of the law, and Garrett regarded Cash warily and none too respectfully. He looked to take seriously his forty-dollar-a-month job as a Wyatt City peace officer.

"Garrett," Cash returned.

"Reckon you know 'bout your brother."

Cash nodded. "Yeah."

"Gonna have to have a word with your mother," he said.

"I'd prefer if you didn't, Garrett," Cash said, explaining as courteously as he could: "Ma hasn't been well. If it's all right with you, I'd like to have a talk with Ethan first."

"You know I've got him locked up."

Cash took a breath and asked, "How bad is it?"

Garrett shifted his weight to his other foot, glanced downward, then shot Cash a direct look in the eye.

"Pretty bad."

"The fella I saw in the alley . . . ," Cash ventured.

"Alive. He's at Doc Pedersen's office. Yeah, he's still breathin'. Might not be for long, though."

"I'll walk back with you," Cash said heavily.

The two men didn't speak as they strolled back into town toward the stone-constructed jailhouse. Cash got the impression that maybe Garrett did have things to say to him, as he was sighing a lot. But Cash was glad he refrained from talk. They'd never been particularly friendly growing up. Garrett was one of the "good kids," while Cash palled around with the likes of Steve Reno. Cash was sure if Garrett had said anything to him, it would have been something he'd rather not hear.

They walked into the jail—and there he was. Cash McCall's kid brother, Ethan, behind bars, sharing a cell with his three friends.

Cash said to Garrett, "Any chance I can talk to my brother alone?"

Garrett looked at him in silence for a moment, considering his request. Cash knew what he was thinking. Let the kid out of his cell, and he and his outlaw brother might make a run for it.

"Think it best if you talk to him just where he is," he finally said.

Cash gave a faint nod and walked over to the far end of the cell, opposite from where Ethan's friends were huddled together on the lower bunk. He jerked his head for his brother to come over.

Ethan slowly shuffled toward him, throwing glances back to his friends. The same kids who were in awe of Cash, the outlaw. Cash could tell it made Ethan feel like quite the big man having his famous brother show up. But he sure as hell wasn't impressing Cash.

Right away Cash noticed a swelling on the side of Ethan's face where he had hit him. Once Ethan stood across from him, he made a deliberate gesture to touch it, wincing at the pain. Cash ignored his obvious try for his sympathy.

"Can you gimme a cigarette?" Ethan asked curtly.

Cash turned to Garrett, seated on the edge of his desk, who nodded, and he rolled the kid a smoke. After Cash lit it for him, he said, "Reckon you never gave no thought to what this would do to Ma."

"It was . . . just a misunderstandin'," Ethan said as he drew heavily on his cigarette.

Cash squinted his eyes dubiously. "Yeah. Well, that *misunderstandin',* as you call it, might just have killed a man."

Ethan seemed unconcerned. "He had it comin'," he said quickly, defensively.

"You ain't that young not to have a rope strung 'round your neck," Cash told him straight.

His harsh words seemed to sober the kid. Cash noted a slight trembling in Ethan's fingers as he pulled another long drag. Then he dropped what was left of the cigarette to the floor and mashed it with his boot heel.

"They—they ain't gonna hang me," he said, trying to sound confident but with a nervous edge to his voice.

"The hell they ain't," one of Ethan's friends piped up, laughing.

The others joined in on the laughter, as did Ethan, obviously wanting to be a part of their bravado, but his laugh was less genuine.

Garrett told them to all quiet down.

Cash just kept staring straight at his brother. "You gonna tell me what happened?" he said.

Ethan turned to his friends, as if looking for their permission. Cash reached a hand through the bars, took his brother by the collar, and slowly turned him back around to face him.

"I'm sure your friends have their own story," he said directly to Ethan. "But I wanna hear yours."

The kid was hesitant.

"Might be smart to practice on me," Cash advised. " 'Cause no matter which way this goes, you'll be tellin' it 'fore a judge."

"Go on, tell him," one of his friends urged. "Hell, he's Cash McCall. He'll understand."

Cash gave the kid a sour look, but if that was the only way he was going to hear what happened, he grudgingly appreciated the recognition.

"I wanna hear you tell how you and your friends near beat a man to death," Cash said with a cold edge to his voice.

"No," Ethan said quickly. "It—it wasn't like that. I went out to get a sarsaparilla, just like I told you. But I ran into some of the fellas, and we decided to go shoot a game of pool. So we get there, and there's this loudmouth shootin' his mouth off 'bout how much money he was winnin'. Well, after he left, me and the guys went out, and he sees us and keeps on boastin' 'bout what a rich guy he is from all his bettin'. We start funnin' him, and he takes it all serious, and next thing any of us knows, he's comin' after us. He . . . he pulled a knife. We hadda fight back."

"We didn't find any knife," Garrett stated.

"It was there. I swear. Ask the fellas."

"I ain't askin' no one," Garrett said bluntly. "There was no knife." He paused, then added slyly, " 'Less one of you young gentlemen took it."

None of the kids spoke. The room became silent.

"If'n that's the case, you'd be wise to fess up," Garrett advised. "Could make a big difference at your trial."

Each of the boys merely hung his head.

Garrett wore a satisfied smile. "That's what I figgered."

Cash shook his head. There was no knife . . . and it looked as if the kids now had no defense.

He spoke a little sadly to his brother. "I hoped maybe you'd learnt somethin' from what I been through. Ain't nothin' I can do for you now."

"I ain't askin' for your help," Ethan suddenly snapped. "You wasn't there for me when I needed you. Why'd I be expectin' anythin' from you now . . . Go on. Just get outta here."

Cash felt sorry for the kid. But Ethan clearly didn't need his sympathy. He had enough of his own self-pity to wallow in.

Cash had just one final thing to say to him—a long shot, maybe, but it might bring out some decency in his brother. "That girl I saw tonight. The one who came runnin' to you . . ."

For just that fraction of a second Ethan's tough-guy facade cracked. Cash noticed a flash of acknowledgment in his eyes. But the spark was swiftly extinguished.

Instead he narrowed his eyes, smirked, and backed away. Alone, maybe Cash could have prodded something out of him. But he was too much the big shot with his friends nearby, sharing his predicament and not one appearing too disturbed about it.

Cash turned and started to walk toward the door. Garrett watched him, his expression hard to read. Was he thinking that maybe Ethan was right—about Cash not being there for him? Or was it more the example Cash had set by venturing into lawlessness? There was truth in the kid's words, no denying it. But Cash couldn't add that burden to all the other guilt he was carrying. Ethan had made his own choices. Just as he had.

Before he left the jailhouse, Cash stopped and looked back at his brother, now mingling among his friends.

Where he chose to belong.

Chapter Four

Ma, of course, had to be told, and, as Cash expected, she was devastated. Cash tried to smooth things over with her as best he could, but the truth of the story was talked about throughout the town, and it wasn't long before she knew all the grisly details.

When the circuit judge arrived in Wyatt City to officiate at the trial, Cash tried to persuade Ma not to go. A lot of things were going to be said that she didn't need to hear. But she was there at the courthouse every day, sobbing frequently and wringing her hands helplessly. The courthouse was crowded—standing room only—and Cash got as many stares from the spectators as did the four defendants. He supposed that some might even have thought he'd live up to his desperado reputation and try to break his brother out with guns blazing.

The victim of the beating had recovered sufficiently to take the stand as the primary witness. He presented a sorry figure, bruised and bandaged, and the story he told naturally contradicted the feeble defense Ethan and his friends had tried on the court. He claimed he had done nothing to provoke the attack, carried no knife, and that the gang just wanted to rob him of his winnings.

His account of the events was believed, and the jury unanimously found the four youths guilty of attempted robbery and assault. All Cash and his mother could hope for now was that the judge would show leniency because of their ages.

But he was not about to do so, especially after observing the tough, cocky attitudes the gang had adopted after they knew their fates were sealed.

They each were sentenced to two years in the Territorial Prison at Huntersfield. It wasn't quite the hellhole that Bennetsville was, but still a rough environment for a wet-nosed kid like Ethan. The one consolation was that prisoners in that institution were taught a profitable skill, and as long as Ethan behaved himself, there was every chance that he could benefit from his experience and come out a better person.

Of course the cards could be turned the other way, and he could emerge as another Steve Reno. Either way, Cash knew that, after two years at Huntersfield, Ethan wouldn't be walking out the kid he knew.

Not more than a week after Cash sat in the courthouse listening to a stern-faced judge hand down Ethan's sentence, he found himself pacing the floors of his house, awaiting a verdict of a different kind.

It was a Sunday, and he'd slept late that morning—a refreshing change from his usual pattern. He figured that the past week had finally caught up with him. Even after he awoke, he didn't rush out of bed, not feeling much incentive to face another day. It was around ten thirty, and by that time Cash expected to hear Ma shuffling around the kitchen, busying herself with preparing breakfast. But this morning the house was unusually quiet. Soon he climbed out of bed and threw on his shirt and pants.

He first looked in the kitchen, hoping that he'd find Ma at the table having her coffee. But she wasn't there, so he turned to look toward her bedroom. The door was still closed. Cash walked over and knocked gently. There was no response. Swallowing his breath, he turned the knob and glanced inside. Ma wasn't in her bed, and Cash thought with a momentary relief that maybe she was feeling well enough to go to Sunday services, which she regularly attended when she was up to it.

Still, he entered the room . . . and as he rounded the side of the bed, he saw Ma lying motionlessly on the floor. Cash quickly crouched beside her and touched her neck for a pulse. Her skin felt cold, but he could feel a faint throbbing. Cash wanted to lift her back onto the bed but thought better about moving her and instead covered her warmly with a blanket. Then he raced out of the house to fetch the doctor.

An anxious Cash urged Doc Pedersen out of his pew at church, understandably startling the physician's wife and the other parishioners. The doctor's buggy was outside, but it was faster to go on foot. They made a quick stop at his office, where Doc Pedersen picked up his medical bag, and then ran the distance back to the house.

The doctor checked Ma and then helped Cash carefully lift her limp body onto the bed. He advised Cash to wait outside the room while he examined her. Cash paced the parlor floor and tried to roll a cigarette, but his hands were unsteady while he again slipped into guilt, contemplating his own role in her sickness. All the stress had been too much for Ma, especially in her weakened condition. Cash put much of the blame on his brother . . . but he blamed himself more. As he saw it, he'd failed Ma by not setting a good example for the kid. Not in the short time that he'd been home from prison, during which he at least tried to put out an effort, but throughout Ethan's entire life, when Cash outright neglected any kind of responsibility. He couldn't undo the mistakes of a lifetime in just a few weeks, and, as he now rationalized, if he'd had any sense, he would have known it was foolish to try.

Time, his enemy, again taunted him as Cash listened to the slow, steady ticking of the wall clock, each passing minute that brought no word from the doctor tightening the knot in his stomach.

Finally Doc Pedersen walked out of the bedroom, gently closing the door partway behind him. The look on his face told Cash all he needed to know. Cash stepped over to him.

"Your mother's a very sick woman," the doctor said gravely.

"Just tell me what's wrong with her," Cash said, working to keep his voice calm.

"Looks like apoplexy." Doc Pedersen paused before going on. "As I told you, she's been ill for a long time, and she's been ignoring it."

"Reckon maybe she hadda," Cash muttered with his eyes lowered.

The doctor gave a slow nod, as if he understood.

"So . . . what are you suggestin' we do?" Cash asked.

"I'm afraid at this point I'm not not 'suggesting,'" the doctor said directly. "It's imperative that we get her the proper medical care. I recommend the County Hospital in Stafford."

Cash squirmed a little. "That'll cost money."

Now it was the doctor's turn to look uncomfortable. "There are special considerations . . . for charity cases."

"No," Cash said flatly.

Doc Pedersen regarded him with a sympathetic expression and spoke softly. "McCall, you might as well know, your mother may not recover. She might not even regain consciousness. And even if she should survive this attack, most likely she'll suffer some permanent impairment. At this point I can't know the severity of her condition. It would be to her benefit—and yours too—if she were in a facility where she can properly be diagnosed and given the right care." He paused, his voice even quieter now. "Or at least be made comfortable."

His words were tinged with the awful helplessness that Cash, too, felt. He wanted to hear just a hint of hope, but what the doctor was saying offered little encouragement.

Cash swallowed past the bile rising in his throat. "You sayin' . . . you don't figger she's gonna make it?"

"I can't say either way for certain, McCall. But, yes, it's possible she may not last out the week. And even that may be an optimistic prognosis."

Cash hardly appreciated the bluntness of Doc Pedersen's words. But he also understood that the doctor had to be up front with him.

"She ain't gonna be no charity case, Doc," Cash repeated firmly.

Doc Pedersen sighed. "Of course. I understand. But whatever you decide, I'd suggest you make the decision quickly."

"I already decided, Doc. How soon till we can get her looked after?"

Doc Pedersen had a skeptical look to him. But he said, "I'll make the arrangements immediately. I'll have to wire Stafford and get them to notify the hospital. We'll have to supply safe transportation, since Stafford is a twenty-mile ride. Until then I can have a woman come by to help out. I know a good woman who's worked with me from time to time." Doc Pedersen pulled his watch fob from his vest pocket and checked the time. "Church has let out by now. I can stop by her house on my way to the telegraph office."

"Reckon you better get on it," Cash said.

And then the reason for Doc Pedersen's doubtful look became clear. "About the cost . . ."

"I'll—I'll take care of the money," Cash said, making himself speak confidently.

Cash silently questioned whether the doctor believed him, but Doc Pedersen could see he was serious and had the courtesy not to ask the whereabouts of his resources.

"All right, McCall, I'll get off that wire."

"'Preciate it, Doc." Cash extended his hand, and the doctor shook it. The grip of his handshake was nearly as feeble as Cash himself felt at the moment.

Doc Pedersen started for the door. But before he turned the knob, he stood still for a brief moment. Without looking back, he said something that Cash reckoned he felt obligated to say:

"Your mother's a good woman, McCall."

He then left the house, and Cash held his own position for a time, not moving, hardly even breathing. The doctor's words stayed with him as he acknowledged the truth in them. His mother *was* a good woman who deserved a hell of a lot more than what life had handed her. Cash thought how unfair it was. Her rewards for all she'd worked for were two sons turned bad and now a sickness that could either kill her or keep her some kind of a bedridden cripple.

Cash stayed in the house while Doc Pedersen went to fetch the woman who would be caring for Ma. Cash hardly knew any of the people in Wyatt City anymore, but he put his trust in the doctor's choice.

He went back into the room and stood at the foot of Ma's bed. It was hard for him to look at her. To see her so sick and helpless. It was a strange kind of a feeling when the person who had spent much of her life taking care of you and staying strong in the face of so many of life's hardships suddenly . . . just wasn't that person anymore.

Shortly the woman arrived, a gray-haired, heavyset widow named Mrs. Brasson. While not a close friend of Ma's, she knew her through church. Cash gave her a quick appraisal and determined that she'd do all right for Ma. Mrs. Brasson went into the bedroom to check on her and when she came out told Cash that his mother seemed to be resting comfortably. She could see the strain on Cash's face and suggested he go out for a while. Take a walk and get some air. Cash appreciated her concern and agreed. The house felt as if it were closing in on him.

Sunday afternoon, and the streets in town were quiet. Cash wandered to the outskirts of Wyatt City and continued down the dirt road that stretched into the open country. He headed west, gazing off into the distance at the sharp blue peaks of the Teton range. He just kept walking—and thinking, his mind a maze with what seemed like a lot of dead ends. He thought about sending a message to Ethan—not out of a sense of responsibility, but to let the kid wallow in his own helplessness, let him assume some of the guilt for what was happening to their mother. But that was the wrong motive; he'd be acting out of spite. And if the kid actually did give a damn, Cash didn't put it past him to do something crazy, like try to break out of prison. Ethan would have to know—Cash realized that—but since there was nothing he could do where he was, Cash decided to wait until he could arrange a visit and tell him something definite.

Definite. When did Cash McCall ever know anything definite? His whole life had been a series of chances, like a roll of the dice in a game of Chuck-a-Luck. Sometimes a lucky combination, most times not. Cash got to thinking about Steve Reno. He'd had his share of bad rolls, yet somehow the guy always seemed lucky to him. Maybe it was his attitude. No matter how tough the breaks, he never surrendered to it. He just kept playing the dice, challenging the odds, always expecting to come out a winner. As for Cash, he'd have been content just to break even. Yet even then he could never seem to beat the odds.

It all boiled up inside of him. Ma was laid up in bed, a prisoner in her frail, sickly body. Ethan was locked away, a prisoner of the state. And Cash was walking in the countryside, a free man. Only he wasn't free. He felt more trapped than either of them. When a man becomes a prisoner of his conscience, he can't be less free than if he was condemned to a life behind bars.

That's how Cash felt. As if the walls were closing in on him tighter than they ever had at Bennetsville.

He had to break free. Suddenly all he wanted was to get away from the town, the memories, everything that was a reminder of who he was . . . and maybe who he had tried to be since leaving prison.

But first—most important of all, even if Ma had only a few days to live—he wanted to give her the care she deserved. And then ride hard and fast to a new start, a new life.

But how could he do any of that without money? He'd had some once. A nice pile of currency courtesy of a farmers' bank in Hensford. Now he didn't even own a horse. Or even his fancy sidearms. All that had been taken from him when he was arrested.

There had to be some answer. There *had* to be. . . .

With his frustration and desperation built up to a fever-boil, Cash saw the one possible solution to his troubles.

Damn the consequences.

And that was when he turned and started running back into town, led on by an urge he wasn't ready to fully acknowledge, yet one that had taken a firm grip on his mind and soul. He hurried back through the dusty streets and up along the boardwalk, his boots hammering hard on the wood planking. He knew where he had to go. Whom he had to see. Maybe he was playing a long shot. He might even change his mind once he got there. But he had to keep running—let impulse and the boardwalk lead him to a decision he convinced himself he had to make.

When he went 'round back to the rear door of the saloon after his long run, Cash was barely sweating. He was hardly short of breath. His state of mind was such that he'd hardly felt any of the exertion. He knew the place was closed, but before he would allow himself even a moment of rational thought, he pounded a fist solidly against the door. Cash knew that Molly roomed in the back of the saloon and that she was there now. She never went anywhere. Her ugliness kept her inside, a virtual hermit.

Soon the door opened a crack, and that hideous face with the deformed right eye peered out at him. Cash didn't give Molly the chance to say anything; he just pushed his way inside.

Molly was startled by his abruptness and swiftly stepped out of his way.

"With all that hammerin' I thought you was the law comin' to close me down," she growled.

Cash started down the corridor adjacent to her small living quarters that led into the saloon. Molly followed him. The front inside doors were closed and locked over the batwings, and the saloon was empty and quiet.

Cash went to the bar, and Molly hobbled behind the counter. She hunched herself over, fiddling with something, and when she rose, Cash saw that she had slipped on her pirate eye patch.

"Ya want me to get you a drink?" she said. "Ya look like you could use one."

Yeah, a drink. That was exactly what he could use.

Cash nodded, and Molly poured him a straight shot of whiskey. She was either in a right cordial mood, or Cash had her scared.

"Here, have one on the house," she offered.

Cash took the glass without thanking her and tossed back the whiskey.

"You in some kinda trouble, McCall?" Molly asked as she went to refill his glass.

Cash put up a hand to stop her. He didn't want to spend the last few dollars he had on alcohol, tempting though the urge was.

"Nah." Molly smiled a ghastly smile that sent a cold shiver through him. "I can stake ya to another one."

He again accepted her hospitality without an acknowledgment.

The two shots worked magic on Cash. He felt warm and easy. He finally spoke his first words to Molly since making his rude entrance.

"Not the kind of trouble you think, Molly. But . . . maybe you can help."

Molly drew out a pre-rolled cigarette from her silver case and offered one to Cash. He accepted, and she lit both smokes. Molly looked at Cash peculiarly, with more than a hint of interest, as though maybe trying to figure how she could profit from his problem. Molly was a woman always on the lookout for the next buck.

"Not that kind of trouble, Molly," Cash repeated, reading her thoughts.

"McCall, you know me," she said, inhaling her cigarette and blowing curls of smoke toward the ceiling. "I don't ask no questions."

She was right about that. Molly could be trusted because she had her own interests to protect.

There were only the two of them in the saloon, but Cash still lowered his voice when he said, "I hear Steve Reno's gettin' out."

Molly's lips parted, and she breathed out the words, "The Whiskey Kid? He's already out."

Molly moved to put the bottle away. Cash stopped her and pulled out some silver. She obliged by filling his glass—and this time she took the money.

"He ain't keepin' himself too visible," Molly added. "But I seen him."

"He been around here?"

Molly nodded. "Some. Usually comes by after closin'."

Cash tried to sound casual when he said, "He . . . ask 'bout me?"

"Your name came up."

Cash downed his third shot. He needed it.

"So . . . you wanna see The Kid?" Molly asked with a note of irony in her voice.

It wasn't hard for Cash to guess why she was speaking in that tone. It had been spread throughout town that bank robber and ex-convict Cash McCall was planning to lead a law-abiding life. Much to his chagrin, his noble intention had been met with suspicious stares and even some whispered mocking by a few of Wyatt City's "decent folk." He was wagering he'd get a similar response if he got the chance to sit down with Steve Reno.

Cash looked up at Molly, slowly, directly into her one good eye. "Yeah," he said.

Molly nodded. "I'll see what I can do, McCall. Like I always said, you're a coupla good boys. Lessee, can you come back tonight? Say, 'bout eleven?"

Eleven o'clock. That meant Cash would have most of the day ahead of him. Time to think. And he couldn't wager a guess on how he'd be thinking come eleven. With the three shots of whiskey relaxing him, he was starting to have doubts already.

"Eleven," Molly repeated. "The Kid'll be here. Him . . . and maybe some of the others."

By "others" Cash knew she meant Slug Fletcher and probably one or two of the neighborhood toughs who were chummy with Steve. Guys who shared Steve's big ideas. That wasn't the way Cash wanted it; he was hoping to speak with Steve alone. But he couldn't tell that to Molly. If he wanted to meet with Steve, he'd have to do it on whatever terms he chose.

Cash gave Molly a brisk nod and left the bar through the back entrance.

The hours went by just as slowly as Cash knew they would. He went back home for a while where he sat quietly in the parlor with Mrs. Brasson, sharing a pot of tea while she sat in the old wood rocker, keeping herself busy with knitting. Ma was still asleep. Mrs. Brasson told Cash that she seemed to be resting comfortably, and then she asked if he would like to look in on her. Cash declined, rather too quickly. He said he didn't want to chance disturbing Ma, that she needed her rest. Mrs. Brasson regarded him with a subtle look that told Cash she suspected otherwise. Maybe she understood.

All Cash knew was that he was feeling pretty low. There was his mother lying helpless in the next room . . . and he just wasn't ready to see her like that again.

Sitting in the quiet with nothing to occupy his thoughts, Cash felt his brain once again start to gallop, like a thirsty horse racing toward an oasis mirage. The doubts were beginning to pile up. He kept trying to push them away by convincing himself that what he was planning was his only chance of helping his mother. He wasn't thinking about himself or the risks that were sure to be there. It was what he had to do. He owed at least that much to Ma.

By suppertime no news had come from Doc Pedersen, and Cash again felt restless and wanted to leave the house. As awful as it might seem, he also didn't want to be there when they took Ma away, so he explained to Mrs. Brasson that he had an urgent appointment that he'd forgotten about and would she see to it when the time came to take Ma to the hospital. She again gave him that curious yet knowing look but agreed. To make her feel a little less unkindly toward him, Cash promised to come by the hospital after Ma was settled. The way he justified it, there wasn't anything he could do for her now except what was most important: get the money to pay for her care.

To pass time and get his mind off any sensible thinking, Cash walked into town and headed into the coffee shop, the Elite Café, which was the only business open at this hour on Sunday night. Wyatt City was a town that pretty much did as it pleased throughout the week but remained respectful on the Sabbath. Those so inclined would have to satisfy themselves with a good drunk on Saturday night, which they could sleep off all the following day, since saloon proprietors respectfully closed their doors come Sunday.

Respectfully? They had little say in it. It was the law. Wyatt City liked to regard itself as a God-fearing community.

Cash took a table next to the big window that overlooked the street. He didn't know how long he sat in the café, but he nursed two cups of coffee and munched on a piece of pie while he waited for the skies to get dark. After a spell he started to notice that he was getting peculiar looks from the waitress. Finally she came over to him and announced, "We close at eight."

Only eight o'clock? It had to be later than that. Cash determined that he had never gone through a slower day in his life, not even in prison. But he checked his pocket watch, and, sure enough, it read ten minutes to eight. He didn't know how to occupy himself for the next three hours. But he had to do something. He could not stay idle and allow those troubling doubts to crawl back into his brain.

It was then that he tossed a casual glance up at the waitress and noticed how she was kind of smiling at him. Not in the professional serve-the-customer way that she had when she'd taken his order. This look seemed to suggest . . . something different.

Cash quickly reasoned that maybe he'd simply been away from a woman too long. But that crooked little smile hinted to him that this gal was hunting for something other than a nickel tip.

He checked her over in the least obvious way he could. She was rather hard looking but in her own way somewhat attractive. Someone who likely once had a lot going for her, before life had plastered a trail map of tough breaks across her face. She had long black hair that she wore bunched up behind her, fastened with a pink ribbon, which, when flowing freely, would frame a face highlighted by pronounced cheekbones and dark-complected skin that suggested she might be of Mexican heritage.

Cash didn't know what she wanted from him, but she sure seemed to be waiting for something—and not being too shy about it. Finally he got up from his chair. Even though he could hardly afford it, he tossed two bits onto the table. She didn't even look at it.

Cash began to walk away. But before he reached the door, he stopped and glanced back at her. He was curious. Maybe she knew who he was, was familiar with his reputation. Like most of the town.

He gave her a polite nod and stepped outside. There he stopped to roll a cigarette, and just moments later the door to the café opened, and the girl came out. She had a shawl wrapped around her shoulders and looked cold, though the night was mild for the season. She stood next to Cash and again wore that puzzling smile.

"Think you could spare one of those?" she said, indicating his cigarette.

Cash shrugged and, though his tobacco was running low, rolled her a thin cigarette. She accepted it in her slight hands and stood there, now expecting him to light it for her. Wordlessly he obliged, striking a match against his boot heel, then holding it in the cup of his other hand against the slight evening breeze. She moved in with her cigarette tucked between pursed lips. As she inhaled, she lifted her brown eyes to meet his, the glow of the match catching both to give her eyes an almost feline look. Then she drew back and exhaled smoothly.

"Thanks," she said.

"Don't mention it," Cash replied.

They stood there under the awning of the café smoking their cigarettes, when what she next said caught Cash unawares.

"I only live a few blocks from here."

Cash arched an eyebrow but didn't respond.

"Not far," she added. "But I always get a little nervous walking home after dark."

An invitation if ever he'd heard one. Cash wasn't so much curious now as downright suspicious. He was thinking that maybe he should just smile, say good night, and turn and walk away. But instead he found himself replying, "You askin' me to walk you home?"

She blew out a fine stream of smoke that billowed into the night. "I'm not asking," she said demurely.

He gave his head a slight, puzzled shake and took her lightly by the arm. "I'll walk with you."

She hardly spoke two words as they strolled the short distance to where she lived. She never even told Cash her name, and he didn't offer his. But he got a bit of a shock once they got to her home.

The house stood alone, off the main road, nestled in a grove of trees and other shrubbery-type growth. It was a white-framed, two-storied structure, the steeply slanted shingled roof adorned with a pair of windowed cupolas. The front porch was wide and shaded by a sloping overhang supported by two solid columns positioned at opposite ends of the house.

Cash grew up in town and was not unfamiliar with the history of the house or its whispered reputation. It once had served as a boarding residence for saloon girls known as much for their after-hour favors as their barroom serving skills, and it was ru- ·

mored that many of the late-night visitors to the house were some of Wyatt City's most established and respected citizens.

An outraged church committee finally closed down the house and ran the girls out of town. After that the house went unoccupied for many years. Cash had never visited the place during its years as a bordello and thought it odd to find himself there now. Especially with a gal who now apparently lived there.

"Would you maybe like to come inside for a drink?" the girl offered.

"Most rooming houses I'm familiar with don't allow male callers after dark." Cash spoke with an intended ignorance to see how she would respond.

"True," she agreed. Then she smiled. "But this isn't a rooming house. I happen to own it."

His eyes slowly veered toward her.

"I know what you're thinking," she said, amused at his bewildered reaction. "Working as a coffee shop waitress and affording a house like this. *This* house. Really it's not so strange."

"Is to me. More'n strange, if you wanna know."

"Well, if you'd care to come in for that drink, we can talk about it."

The way it seemed to Cash, the whole day had felt as if someone else had been living it and he was just an observer to all the strangeness. His odd meeting with this girl only added to it. But he decided to accept her invitation, thinking it might not be the worst way to get through the next couple of hours.

They went inside, and Cash stood back in the entrance hall while she went into the parlor to light the kerosene in the glass-shaded, crystal-fringed table lamps. When the room was sufficiently lit, Cash peered inside and looked with awe at the expensive furnishings and other elegant knickknacks that decorated the place. Her owning the house, maybe, was one thing. But these other possessions had to cost far more than what she could earn serving coffee and pie. Cash reached an immediate and definite conclusion. The history of this old house was repeating itself. This gal clearly had a neat little sideline going.

Cash didn't hold that against her. But he wasn't in any financial position to add to her comforts. He wanted to tell her just that, only his pride held him back. He also didn't want to come across as crude on the off chance this wasn't a "business arrangement."

He stood outside the parlor while she disappeared into another room, most likely to change out of her pink waitressing uniform. Cash was feeling mighty awkward and considered just sneaking out through the door.

Then her voice called out, "Don't just stand out in the hall. Come inside and make yourself comfortable."

Cash declined. "'Fraid I really can't stay. I, uh, have to meet with a friend."

"Not even time for a drink? A short one."

He kept thinking he should just skedaddle, then and there. But the offer of liquor tempted him to stay. Knowing what was coming up later tonight, a drink would go down good.

"Help yourself," she called out. "There's a bottle in the kitchen cupboard. Glasses are on the counter."

Cash walked down the end of the hall to where he saw the kitchen opened. He found an unopened bottle of whiskey and half filled two glasses. He downed his drink in a quick, single swallow, then poured in some more. It was stinging corn liquor that burned its way down his throat and had a savage kick. He felt it buzzing around in his head instantly and realized he'd be smart to take it easy.

He carried the glasses into the parlor and placed hers on the coffee table next to a richly upholstered sofa that could comfortably seat two. But he chose the rocker across the room. His head had stopped swirling from that first swig of liquor, and now, as he sipped his drink, he was feeling a nice, warm glow and was relaxed.

Maybe too relaxed. Because that was when it happened.

Was it the corn whiskey or his being alone with a woman for the first time in years? Cash wasn't sure, but he began to seriously question her intentions and wasn't comfortable with what he saw as the possible outcome. Those feelings that prison had forced him to long suppress came rushing at him like a tidal wave. He struggled to keep his thoughts focused in another direction, even conjuring up the gruesome image of Dead Eye Molly to settle his "restlessness," but his valiant efforts were quickly losing out to a surge of physical needs that had never been so strong. If she *did* have something else in mind beyond just sharing a friendly drink, Cash wasn't sure he was ready for it.

On the other hand, maybe he was *too* ready.

And that decided it for him. His hoped-for diversion lasted long enough for him to swallow two glasses of corn whiskey. Before he even had time to remove his cowboy hat, he was gone out the door.

He walked along the streets, feeling a sense of relief. Maybe a bit of guilt at his fast departure, but he reminded himself that he owed her no obligation. Hell, he didn't even know her name. Besides, he had more important matters to deal with.

While there was still time to back out, Cash was determined to keep his appointment with Steve Reno.

He wandered through the late-night quietness of the town until it finally neared eleven o'clock. Then he waited outside of Dead Eye Molly's for about another fifteen minutes. Strangely, during that time he never saw Steve or any of the boys show up. They were either late . . . or had already gotten there. Or maybe they weren't going to show. Cash truthfully didn't know how he felt about that last possibility.

But exactly at the time the hands on his pocket watch reached the hour, he was at the back entrance. Cash drew in and exhaled a deep, calming breath, then lightly knocked on the door. He had to admit, he was somewhat apprehensive. Maybe Steve Reno was a longtime pal, but he had doubts the guy he was meeting tonight would be someone he'd recognize.

The door slowly opened. Cash was expecting to see Molly on the other side, but the face that greeted him belonged to some guy he'd never seen before: a tough-looking, dark-skinned hombre, possibly an Indian or half-breed, with hooded eyes and long, greasy black hair streaming out from under his straw cowboy hat. He didn't say a word to Cash, though he studied him pretty closely.

"I'm McCall," Cash said. "I'm here to see Steve Reno."

Then the door opened all the way, and Cash walked inside.

The dark-skinned man gave his head a jerk to gesture Cash toward the saloon.

Cash walked through the corridor and stepped into the dimly lit room.

"You're right on time, compadre."

Steve Reno sat almost as a shadow at a dark corner table. Two other men were with him. Cash wasn't surprised to see Slug Fletcher. Nobody could have mistaken him. As he walked in closer, he also recognized Chester McGraw, whom he remembered simply as "Chick," one of his boyhood chums. Cash still didn't know who the Indian was—who, he noticed with almost a start, was following closely behind him. So closely, in fact, that it made Cash uneasy, thinking the man was getting ready to plunge a knife into his back.

The first thing Cash noticed was that his pal Steve hadn't changed much in the months since he'd last seen him. That might not seem significant, until one considered the conditions at Bennetsville. Cash remembered seeing men deteriorate into physical wrecks within a couple of weeks of their confinement. Maybe Steve was a bit thinner, which further accentuated his hawklike profile, and his face had a pale complexion that might have been more the result of the low lighting in the saloon. But overall it was evident that his stay in Bennetsville hadn't disagreed with him. Or apparently changed his cheerful mood.

He was still impeccably groomed and well dressed, wearing a brocade vest over a freshly laundered white shirt. A handsome, cream-colored Stetson with a black band was resting next to him on the table.

"Take yourself a chair," he invited. "Just out of prison, and it already feels like a hometown reunion."

The saloon was heavy with cigar smoke. Not a cheap, unpleasant smell. All the guys at the table were sucking on fat cigars. Before Cash could even seat himself, Steve pushed a decorated box across the table toward him.

"Imported," Steve explained.

Cash lifted a cigar from the box and sniffed it, giving an approving nod before tucking it into his breast pocket. "I'll save it for later," he said, instead rolling a cigarette with the few flakes of tobacco remaining in his pouch.

"The night's on me, compadre," Steve announced. "Anythin' you want."

Cash took a chair directly across from Steve, with Slug Fletcher and Chick McGraw sitting on either side. Slug ignored him, his interest focused on a large, sloppy plate of food that might have been sow belly, sourdough, and beans. Chick just stared at Cash intently, slowly rolling his cigar from one side of his mouth to the other. They'd never been the closest of friends growing up.

Cash noticed there were two other supper plates laid out before Steve and Chick. They'd already eaten, while Slug was gorging himself on what was probably his second or third helping. That told Cash they'd arrived at Molly's long before eleven.

"You hungry, Cash? Or can I start you off with a drink?" Steve asked.

Cash declined the meal. Even if his stomach hadn't been unsettled, he couldn't have any appetite watching Slug wolf down his strange supper concoction.

But he could certainly use a liquid boost and pointed to the bottle of whiskey on the table.

Steve reached for the bottle and poured him a generous glassful. "Got Molly to bring us a bottle of the good stuff. Not that rotgut she serves her customers."

Steve handed Cash the glass, refilled his own, then raised it in a salute.

Cash halfheartedly lifted his glass and took a swallow. It was good, smooth whiskey.

"Where *is* Molly?" he then asked.

"Drunk in her room in back," Steve answered slyly. "Figgered you'd want this get-together to be private."

Cash glanced at Slug and Chick, then gave a cautious look over to the Indian, who was standing quietly against the wall, watching him.

Steve grinned. "The boys are okay."

Cash thought otherwise. But he wasn't in a position to argue. He needed Steve's help, and, like it or not, Steve's friends would be part of the deal.

"Who's the quiet one?" Cash asked, jerking his head toward the Indian.

"Yeah," Steve said. "You guys haven't met. Cash, meet Andy Chelsea."

Cash took another look at Andy, and the Indian looked back at him with as cold an expression as Cash had ever seen, as if he was considering whether or not to scalp him. Neither spoke to the other.

"Andy got out of Bennetsville 'bout a month ago," Steve explained. "Surprised you never saw him 'round the place."

The way the guy moved, almost without being seen, like a ghost or a shadow, and his eerie silence made Cash think it would be easy for him not to have noticed him. And if he had, Cash would have kept himself at a safe distance.

"He was in on a murder charge," Steve went on. "Woulda hanged him, but some 'witnesses' came forward and said the killin' was in self-defense. 'Cause he's an Injun, they still kept him locked away for a coupla years. For the public good."

Cash nodded absently and returned to his drink. All he knew was that in just these few moments this Andy Chelsea person had proven himself the only other guy besides Slug Fletcher who could really make him nervous.

Steve leaned back in his chair. "Reckon you're surprised to see me out."

Cash didn't answer. Though in truth, nothing surprised him about Steve Reno.

"Guess we can say it's to your benefit," Steve said. "Yeah, I heard 'bout your troubles."

Cash looked at Steve curiously, not expecting to hear that he knew what was going on in his life.

"Territorial Prison. Tough place for a kid. 'Specially if you ain't got much backbone." Steve paused and said in a slow, almost taunting voice, "Ethan got any backbone, compadre?"

Cash didn't care for Reno's words and what they insinuated, and, instinctively, he found himself starting to rise tensely from his chair. That was when Slug Fletcher paid his first notice of Cash, slowly raising and turning his grim eyes toward him. His expression was flat but threatening.

"Siddown, Cash," Steve said calmly.

Cash did, then took a few seconds to relax himself.

Steve offered a friendly smile. "I didn't mean nothin' by it, compadre," he said. "But we both know 'bout prison."

Cash gave a quick nod. Steve wore a satisfied expression and splashed some more whiskey into his glass. Cash glanced over at Slug. He was back to wolfing down his food as though nothing had happened.

"And your ma—that's real tough," Steve said, lowering his head and giving it a sympathetic shake.

Cash wasn't sure if it was a sincere gesture of compassion.

He couldn't finish his drink and put the glass down. The liquor was hitting him pretty hard, not helped by the tension that permeated the room. That was when he noticed that the look on Steve's face wasn't so friendly now. There was a dark cast over his expression, made more intense by the low lighting in the saloon. And when he next spoke, the change in his mood was made even more evident.

"So what is it you want from me, Cash?" he said.

Cash found he couldn't reply.

"Tough to ask a favor," Steve said.

He waited for Cash to speak, but the words still wouldn't come. Cash slowly began to understand what was holding him back. Once he spoke up . . . he was committing to a deal with the devil.

The silence in the room was deafening. Cash's head was starting to pound from it.

Steve leaned forward in his chair. "I'll make it easy for you," he said. "You need money and think I might be able to help you."

"Yeah," Cash finally managed to say in a voice just above a whisper.

Steve settled back in his chair, his expression thoughtful.

"Mebbe I can do somethin'," he said, nodding his head. "But the word I got is that you wanna go straight. Be a law-abidin' citizen."

Cash wouldn't offer Steve what he knew his old friend wanted to hear. And it didn't matter, since Steve soon spoke the words for him.

"Nice plan. But it don't work for guys like us."

"No, it don't," Cash said heavily.

Steve seemed satisfied. "That's good. I just want there to be an understandin' 'tween us. Now we can talk business."

Steve had gotten what he wanted out of his former partner. He got Cash to admit that he was a fool to think he could benefit from an honest life after his outlaw past and serving time in prison.

What troubled Cash McCall was, he'd come to believe that maybe Steve was right.

Chapter Five

The meeting with Steve had been a short one. Cash figured it was merely a preliminary—to give Steve the chance to decide whether he'd ripened enough to join him in the next phase of his criminal career. Past friendships didn't mean a thing where his ambitions were concerned. But Cash reckoned he'd passed his scrutiny; rather, the desperate nature of his situation did. Cash's suspicion that some influential "friends" had had a hand in obtaining Steve's early release from Bennetsville was also confirmed at the meeting. He called them his "partners." Steve revealed that he had been hired to do an important job by these people that guaranteed a rich payday. After some talk he said that he thought he could work Cash into the deal. To bond the arrangement, Steve handed him fifty dollars as an advance, explaining that the partners who were bankrolling this undertaking had provided him with some up-front cash. That was about all that Steve would say. He wouldn't let on who was behind this arrangement. Maybe even he didn't know.

So Cash McCall would once again be riding alongside Steve Reno, the self-proclaimed Whiskey Kid. But it was understood that this wasn't going to be like old times. There would be no partnership with Steve. Cash would be working for him—as one of his gang.

Now that Steve had generously handed him some cash, Cash could put money toward Ma's hospital care. By the time he got home from Dead Eye Molly's after midnight, he noticed that Ma was gone from her bed. There was a scribbled note from Mrs. Brasson informing him that a carriage had arrived and that Ma was on her way to the County Hospital at Stafford. Cash was relieved.

Still, unable to sleep, he sat up for most of the night, then hurried to Doc Pedersen's office first thing in the morning. The doctor wasn't yet at his office, so Cash waited outside for him to arrive. When he did and the two men went inside the waiting room of the small office, the doctor told Cash that he'd just received a telegram confirming that his mother had arrived safely at the hospital, though her condition hadn't improved.

Doc Pedersen again spoke formally, professionally, and advised Cash that he shouldn't get his hopes up for her recovery. But, he added, she was where she needed to be. Cash asked the doctor if he wouldn't mind handling the financial business with the hospital. He agreed, and Cash gave him forty of the fifty dollars to wire Stafford, holding back ten dollars for his own expenses. Doc Pedersen took the money, regarding Cash somewhat suspiciously, but he didn't question how Cash had come by it. Cash then told him to make sure that everything stayed well with Ma. There'd be more money coming.

Doc Pedersen didn't ask *when* but *if* Cash was planning to ride out to see his mother. Cash didn't appreciate the tone of the question until the doctor quietly added that time might be short and that he shouldn't wait too long, and Cash told him that he'd be out to see her soon. He just had a few things to take care of first. That comment also seemed to arouse the doctor's unspoken curiosity.

Cash had another meeting set with Steve for noon, at the Mountainview Hotel, the most fancy and expensive rooming accommodation in Wyatt City. Maybe even in the state of Wyoming.

When he got there, Cash could see how far Steve had come. The world where he now resided was as far removed from their poor shantytown upbringing as if to exist on a different planet. From the moment he stepped inside the clean, spacious, and ornate lobby, Cash envied his friend. It was a luxury so unfamiliar to him that he felt like a trespasser just entering the premises. He walked over to the newfangled passenger lift called an Otis and gazed at the marvel of the contraption. He stepped inside the compartment, and the uniformed operator said, "What floor, sir?" Cash was impressed.

He knew it was just a professional courtesy, but he wasn't used to being spoken to with such respect.

Steve's room was on the top floor of the six-story building. When Cash got out of the passenger lift, he walked the thickly carpeted hallway toward Room 610, at the end of the corridor. He listened to some hushed talking going on behind the door. Then he drew a breath and knocked three short knocks, as Steve had instructed. Shortly, he heard footsteps inside the room approaching the door.

The door was answered by the Indian, Andy Chelsea, wearing a flaming red flannel shirt, who again regarded Cash with a blank look under hooded eyes. He motioned with a jerk of his head for Cash to come inside, then closed the door. Cash glanced over his shoulder to see if the Indian was following shadow-close as he had the night before at the saloon. He was.

Cash looked around the room and was impressed. It was a big suite and finely furnished with pieces that looked to be of some fancy European design. For a guy just out of prison, Steve was living mighty well. Steve, Slug Fletcher, and Chick McGraw were all seated at a big round table, playing cards.

Steve looked up from his hand and greeted Cash expansively. "Glad to see you, compadre. What do you think of my place? Won't even tell you what it costs me to live here." He paused, then could not help himself. "What the hell, hundred a week."

"Swell," was all Cash could say.

Steve shrugged. "Yeah. It'll do—for now."

That was an odd comment. If it had come from anyone else, it might have been seen as boasting. But with Steve Reno, Cash knew he meant it. This place was just the first step up for him, and he wanted Cash to know it.

Steve shot Cash a look in the eye and said, "You know, compadre, once our job is done, there ain't no reason you can't be enjoyin' some of life's luxuries."

"I got a few other obligations to take care of first," Cash said.

"Yeah, I know. Take care of the family. I admire you for that, truly do."

Steve told Slug to deal him out. He got up from the table and walked over to Cash, draping an arm around his shoulder in a friendly fashion. He spoke quietly. "Should tell you, I can't fix nothin' for your brother. He'll have to do his stretch. But I don't want you or your ma to worry 'bout it. I told my partners you're a friend of mine, and they gave me their word they'll take care of things so Ethan won't have no trouble."

"Yeah?" Cash said a little doubtfully.

Steve spoke with assurance. "You can count on it."

"Hope to have the chance to meet your partners," Cash said, adding, "I'm obliged to 'em."

"Just might be arranged," Steve said with a grin.

Steve guided Cash into the bedroom, away from the others. He closed the door partway so they could talk in private.

"Want you to know, I'm glad you're thinkin' our way, Cash," he said. "Coupla the boys still ain't sure we can trust you, since you was plannin' to go honest after leavin' Bennetsville. But we're the best friends you got right now. I think you can see that."

Cash could—though maybe he didn't want to. But how could he argue with all that he saw around him? Steve had stuck to his path and was living in a style Cash could only dream about. As for himself . . . he had tried to go straight, and all his attempts at leading a clean, law-abiding life had only ground him deeper into the dirt. Humbling himself in a futile effort to obtain the most menial of employment. If he continued along that road, his mother would likely die or, at the very least, live out her days in pain and misery because he couldn't afford to pay for her proper care. And Cash couldn't guess what would become of his brother.

But now, by his earning money the only way he could, Ma would get the best care and at least had a chance to get better, and Cash had Steve's assurance that Ethan would be taken care of while serving out his time at Huntersfield.

Maybe he wasn't proud that it had come to this. Maybe he even should have hated himself. But what Cash could not deny was that almost from the day he'd walked out of Bennetsville, he'd become angry and embittered at a system he'd foolishly tried to fit himself back into. He'd done his time, paid his debt to society with sweat and blood, but quickly saw how unforgiving "decent" people could be. He saw it every time he set out looking for a job . . . or even when he took a casual stroll through town. Cash McCall was looked upon as an outlaw, an ex-convict.

If that was the brand they'd chosen to stamp on him, why shouldn't he give the good people of Wyatt City what they expected?

It was self-pitying reasoning. But it was all Cash had to justify his being in that hotel suite with Steve Reno.

He and Steve walked back into the main room. Steve said to the others, "Okay, it's set. McCall is in with us."

His rather grandly stated announcement made no impression on the men, who, except for Andy Chelsea, standing off against a far wall, were still seated at the table, concentrating on their poker playing.

"Anyone got somethin' to say?" Steve said.

Cash wouldn't expect a reply from either Andy or Slug Fletcher, who had a sullen expression on his face as he studied his cards. So Steve looked straight at Chick, who shrugged his shoulders and said tonelessly, "Don't make no never mind to me."

Steve pointed Cash to a chair at the table, and Cash sat down next to Slug. Steve moved across to his own place while Andy remained standing like a vigilant guard. Cash tried to push back his uneasiness as he quickly soaked in the repressed violence that seemed to spill out of Slug and Andy like a poison.

Slug grunted and pulled out a cigar. He chewed off the end and spit it onto the expensive carpeting, then jammed the cigar between his blubbery lips and searched his pockets for a match. Cash obliged by striking one of his own matches against his thumb and lighting it for him. Slug just gave another grunt.

Finally Steve spoke. For emphasis, he pulled out his chair and lifted his left foot onto the seat so that he stood tall over his men.

"Okay, boys, now that we're all here, we can get down to business. I just wanna start by sayin' never mind who's fixin' this deal. Not that they'd mean anythin' to you, but my partners wanna keep themselves shadows. So don't be concernin' yourselves over that."

When no one objected, Steve went on. "What I can tell you is that when I was in Bennetsville, I got hooked up with a fella who'd heard of my reputation and who thought that I could put together a gang of good men for some big shots he had dealin's with. Had some special meetings with their lawyer, and we mapped out the details on the inside.

"A week come Wednesday a Wells Fargo stage will be passin' through outside of town, carryin' boxes that my partners don't want to see reach their destination. It's a transfer of gold worth about a quarter million dollars that's headed in secret to Laramie to help finance the buildin' of a coupla fancy new gambling establishments. My partners own most of the saloons and gamblin' interests along the Laramie strip, and they don't want no competition. But these other fellas have some pretty serious backin' from Nevada and Arizona. They wanna expand their interests. Thing is, if the shipment gets waylaid by a band of desperados and don't arrive, there won't be no further financin', and my partners keep hold of their monopoly.

"As I said, no one knows 'bout the delivery of this gold. There's gonna be a pair of detectives ridin' along, posin' as passengers, from the Beckerman Agency. Now I can tell you my partners own that agency, so while these detectives might have to pretend to put up a bit of a fuss to make it look good, we don't have to worry 'bout them steppin' too much outta line . . . 'ceptin' we gotta kill one of 'em. That's so no one'll later suspect the Beckerman people had a part in this.

"Our only problem might be with the driver and shotgun messenger—and they ain't no concern at all. 'Cause they ain't gonna be ridin' back. Won't be leavin' no witnesses, 'ceptin' our one detective. They both know of the plan but not the double-cross to one of 'em. The one we decide to keep breathin' will be generously compensated for cooperatin'. The way I see it, just keepin' him free of a bullet should be payment enough, but those are the orders, and that's the way we play it. We'll have to lay low for a spell afterward, but my partners have lined up a coupla skinners who'll be blamed for the robbery. With the detective's identification and no one around to dispute his claim, those boys'll be dancin' off a rope, and we'll be scot-free."

"These skinners . . . they don't know they're bein set up?" Chick asked, quietly amused at the thought.

"Know nothin' 'bout it," Steve answered with a grin.

As Cash listened to Steve outlining the plan, he felt a tight clenching at his belly. He was expecting a robbery of some sort—after all, that was the reputation Steve Reno had—but he hadn't counted on there being any killing. But he kept quiet as he listened and was especially careful not to let any hint of doubt show on his face.

"Sounds like a good plan," Chick said. "What's our haul?"

"How does twenty thousand apiece sound?" Steve said with a glint of greed showing in his eyes.

"Sounds . . . good," Chick answered agreeably. "What 'bout supplies?"

"No special firepower," Steve said. "No rifles or eight-gauges. Nothin' too heavy. Sidearms will service us just fine. Everything's provided for, including the horses and the wagon we'll need to get them boxes to our hideout. Chick, you'll be in charge of that. You'll be waitin' outta sight near the spot where we waylay the stage."

"Where's this hideout you're talkin' 'bout?" Chick asked.

"It's a good spot. We'll make a trip out there in a few days." Steve tapped a forefinger against the side of his head. "Memorize the location, 'cause it ain't so easy to find. We'll be meetin' there 'fore the holdup and head right back after we're through."

Slug Fletcher finally spoke in his raspy voice. "What 'bout Molly?"

Steve looked at him dully. "What 'bout her?"

"She get a cut?"

"Yeah," Chick broke in. "Usually does."

"For what?" Steve said angrily. "That old harridan thinks she's entitled to a piece of all the action that goes on 'round Wyatt."

"Sure," Chick said, idly flipping his playing cards through his fingers. "That's 'cause she seems to know 'bout all that goes on."

"Yeah . . . well, Molly don't know nothin' 'bout this," Steve said with intensity. "And she'd best be smart enough to keep her mouth shut if'n she does get to knowin'."

"Molly ain't never too quiet when it comes to money she thinks she's got comin' to her," Chick said musingly.

"That'll be her choice," Steve said flatly.

There was no mystery to what he meant by that comment.

Afterward Steve called Cash aside, out of earshot of the others. Slug and Chick had returned to their card playing, and Andy Chelsea was . . . just stalking about.

"So, Cash, what d'you think?" Steve asked. "You was pretty quiet at the table."

"Just mullin' things over," Cash replied.

Steve's cold, steely eyes were on him tightly. Cash could see he was waiting for him to say more.

"Just didn't expect no killin'," he finally admitted.

Steve nodded, as if he'd expected him to express that concern. "That's how it's gotta be," he said plainly. "It's what keeps us in the clear, so's no one other than that detective can be a witness." Still noticing the uncertainty that Cash wasn't hiding very well, he added with a short laugh, "You don't got to worry 'bout gettin' blood on your hands, compadre. Why'd you think I brought Slug and Andy into the gang?"

Cash exhaled a breath. "I figgered as much."

"Lemme feed you some facts," Steve said. "This job they're wantin' us to do is only what you call a . . . preparation. To see how well we carry it through. They promise to have bigger plans for us. You think I got sprung from Bennetsville just for a chicken-feed holdup? If'n that was the case, they coulda easily got themselves a coupla punks with six-shooters. No, compadre, they need guys with guts. Guys they can trust to do the job just the way they want it done. No mistakes. Can't tell you all yet, but my partners got us in mind for a good future—if'n we come through for them." He added with emphasis, "And that's what I plan to do."

Cash gave his head a slow, thoughtful nod.

Steve continued staring into him. Then he said, "So, you still in with us?"

The question might have sounded funny if the situation

weren't so damn serious. Cash's brain worked with a keen precision. How did Steve think he was going to answer him? He knew the plan—almost every detail. Did Steve really think he was going to tell him he wanted out? Just shake hands—no hard feelings and good luck? No—it was forget friendship, and here's a bullet between the eyes.

He had willingly walked through that door. Whether he wanted to be or not, Cash was now in for the whole ride.

Chapter Six

Cash waited out the week, filling in the time between regular meetings with Steve by checking on Ma's progress with Doc Pedersen. The doctor asked again *if* Cash would be going out to see her, and Cash kept stalling, much to the doctor's discomfiture. But the good news was that she seemed to be holding steady, and there had been no turns for the worse.

The bad news was that if Ma was going to live, she would need continued hospital care, which meant that Cash had to stay committed to Steve and his plan. There was a moment when a voice inside his head whispered that it might have been better all around if Ma hadn't survived her attack. Cash quickly pushed that terrible thought out of his brain.

He'd had to borrow a little extra money from Steve to see him through the next several days, and that weekend he decided to take a stage out to the Territorial Prison at Huntersfield to visit his brother. It was a long ride, more than half a day's journey, but Cash enjoyed getting out into the country and, mostly, away from Steve and the others.

He arrived in town on Friday night. He checked in at a hotel and made arrangements with the livery stable for a horse to ride out to the prison on Saturday, which was the scheduled day for visitors, though restricted to family and lawyers.

He bought himself a bottle at the saloon down the street, brought it up to his hotel room, and drank what he hoped would be enough to put him out for the night. But as usual, sleep didn't come easy. Among other things parading through his brain, Cash kept thinking about his brother and who it would be that he was going to meet once he saw him.

Would it be a swaggering tough, already hardened by prison life?

Or, as Cash was desperately hoping, someone who had been set on the straight, sobered by his experience with the *real* roughnecks and the disciplinary conditions behind the high walls?

The Territorial Prison at Huntersfield reminded Cash a lot of Bennetsville. Too much, in fact, and because of that he felt a familiar discomfort as he sat waiting on the long wooden bench at the long wooden table for his brother to appear on the other side of the wire mesh partition. Guards were stationed around the visiting area, but Cash took quick notice of how the one who covered his corner seemed to stand by extra close. It seemed that Cash McCall's reputation had even reached into Huntersfield.

Ethan didn't seem too pleased to see his brother. He looked well enough, considering, but Cash soon found that his outward appearance wasn't a true show of what he had going on inside him.

Once Ethan was seated across from Cash, he locked his narrowed eyes onto his brother and spewed out his resentment.

"You dirty, low-down . . . why didn't you let me know 'bout Ma?" He kept his voice low, but his tone was full of spit and vinegar.

Cash just looked patiently at him and waited for him to get it all out.

"Yeah, I hadda hear 'bout her bein' sick from a letter the doctor sent to this crummy place."

"Wish he hadn't done that," Cash said calmly.

Ethan's lips tightened. "How come?"

"Felt you had enough to deal with," Cash explained. "Just wanted to give it some time."

"Yeah, well, she's my ma too, Cash," Ethan said, jabbing a finger that poked at the mesh. "What if she'd died, huh? Would you have kept that from me while I rotted in this stinking hole?"

Cash tried to soothe the kid. "She ain't gonna die. 'Fact, the doc says she's showin' some improvement." He spoke his words with all the confidence he could muster. Of course he wasn't being completely honest, but he felt that for Ethan's own good he had to give the kid some encouragement.

"You been out to see her?" Ethan asked, his belligerent attitude starting to ease.

"Will be."

Ethan quieted, and Cash decided it might be wise to change the subject.

"How're *you* doin'?"

Ethan took a breath, exhaled, then did the same again, as if trying to clear the residual hostility from his mood. "All right, I reckon."

"They treatin' you okay?"

"Sure," Ethan said with a sneer. Then he added with some bite, "Anyways, probably better'n you had it at Bennetsville."

Cash nodded with his lips in a tight smile. There was little doubt of that.

Ethan didn't seem any the worse for wear, so Cash figured Steve Reno had been up front when he said Ethan would be taken care of. Again that was one he felt he owed Steve—much to his regret.

"How *you* been gettin' on?" Ethan asked. His tone suggested no real interest.

Cash nodded again and made himself look as sincere as he could.

Ethan shifted a bit on the bench. "And . . . you ain't lyin' to me 'bout Ma?"

"'Course not," Cash lied.

Cash felt awkward with the kid. And he suspected Ethan felt the same way with him. Cash was reminded that they had never been particularly close as brothers and that their individual circumstances had now created a gap that almost made them like strangers.

Cash drew a sigh. "Reckon I should be headin' back."

"To Wyatt?"

"Tonight."

"Yeah, well, I . . . I got some readin' to do," Ethan said. "If we behave, they give us books to read that'll help make us better citizens when we get out." He spoke that last sentence with a sarcastic edge.

Cash didn't believe him, naturally. Not about there being books, but that he was actually reading them. But he understood.

"Lotsa time for it," Cash remarked. "I got more education outta my six years at Bennetsville than I ever did in a classroom."

They looked at each other through the wire mesh in silence. Then they exchanged strained good-byes. Cash left one way and Ethan the other, accompanied by a guard.

Walking from the prison, Cash was embarrassed to admit that he was relieved their visit was over.

Sunday was a long day. Cash had too much time on his hands and, with that, too much time to think. He desperately needed something other than what was fast approaching to occupy his thoughts. He was still plagued by a gnawing uncertainty. He'd managed to keep a rein on those doubts when he met with Steve and the gang, but they were always present and at the forefront of his thoughts.

Cash knew it was wrong, that he was making a mistake that, one way or the other, he would come to regret. He would then try to counter those doubts by making himself believe that it was his *thinking* that was wrong. That it was what he *had* to do—for Ma—and that everything would turn out just as Steve said it would. He conveniently ignored the fact that Steve Reno was a convincing talker.

Cash finally decided that the only way he could relax his thoughts was with some companionship. He needed to be with someone who could help him forget what was ahead. He didn't know how it occurred to him, but one person instantly came to mind.

Strangely, it was a week to the day that he'd first met her—the waitress at the Elite Café, whose name Cash didn't know. He thought he'd take a chance and mosey down to the coffee shop just before closing. He didn't know how she'd take to seeing him after the way he'd so abruptly walked out on her. But he figured he had nothing to lose.

This time Cash didn't go into the café, even though he could have used a hot cup of coffee. The night air had a definite chill.

He stood out of sight next to the big window with the painted lettering and peered inside. All he could see was Sam, the owner, wiping down the serving counter. Cash built himself a cigarette and matched it inside the cup of his hand. He had the brim of his Stetson pulled down low and would have looked mighty suspicious to any passerby who might come along.

Cash checked the time on his pocket watch and saw that it was close to eight o'clock, the Sunday night closing time. He still hadn't seen the girl and wondered if she might not be working tonight. Growing disappointed after a spell, he started to walk away from the window . . . when he caught a side glance of her stepping from the kitchen through the swinging doors. She was wearing her pink waitressing uniform and looked every bit as weather-beaten as Cash remembered.

Still, he couldn't help smiling when he saw her.

Cash finished his cigarette and, without thinking, started to build another. He was feeling anxious. He stepped back into the shadows at the corner of the building once he saw the table lights go out, and moments later the door opened, and both Sam and the girl walked outside. She was wearing the same shawl as before over her shoulders.

She and Sam spoke for a bit before he turned and walked off in the other direction. The girl started toward where Cash was standing, and he held back until she was just a few steps away from him. Then he sauntered out onto the boardwalk.

She was startled. But only for a moment, until she recognized him.

Cash tipped the brim of his hat in a gentlemanly fashion. "Recalled what you said 'bout not likin' to walk these streets at night." He tried not to sound as awkward as he felt he probably looked.

She shook her head, as if in a daze. "I confess, I never expected to see *you* again."

"Yeah, well, I acted pretty rude last week. Least I coulda done was give you an explanation for my runnin' out like that."

She gave Cash a coy, knowing smile. "I kind of had it figured out."

"No," Cash said quickly, anticipating what she was thinking. "It wasn't that. Or—maybe it was at first. I just . . ." He was stumbling over his words like a cowboy who'd been out on the trail too long.

She finished for him, her smile widening. "Felt uncomfortable?"

Cash shrugged and shifted his weight to his other foot. "I hadda be somewhere, and I was late," he said simply.

She gave a faint nod.

"Look," he said. "Least I can do to make it up to you is see you home."

She held her smile. "I'd like that."

It was a clear night, and the moon was out and full and looked like a silver dollar glued against a deepening blue backdrop. The streets were quiet as they usually were on a Sunday night, and it was just the two of them. Strangely, for the first time in a long while Cash was feeling pretty good.

She wasn't the type of girl he was normally attracted to. She wasn't soft-faced pretty. Nor did she have that sweet, rather naïve innocence he'd always found appealing in a female. No, she was hard-looking and clearly a little rough around the edges. A gal who knew something about life. But what Cash noticed during those few moments speaking with her outside the coffee shop was that she had a quality that made up for what he saw as her shortcomings. She had a kind and understanding heart.

Cash realized with some embarrassment that he had misjudged her that first night they met. And he was determined that whatever happened tonight, he would not make another fool of himself.

As they turned the corner leading to her big house, Cash said, "Don't you think we should introduce ourselves?"

She looked thoughtful and then said playfully, "We could. Or we could keep the mystery."

Cash smiled broadly—the first genuine smile he'd given to anyone in a long time.

She held out her hand. "My name's Lucinda."

"Figgered you for a Mexican," he said, and he instantly regretted his quick, stupid comment.

"Half-Mexican, on my mother's side," Lucinda offered,

unoffended at his bluntness. "Verdugo. My father's name is Gee. Shortened from McGee. That's Scottish."

Cash gently met her hand, curling his thick fingers around her slender ones. Then he hesitated. It suddenly occurred to him that she might recognize his name, and, if so, how would she respond?

"Well?" she said, feigning impatience.

"Huh?" Cash was stalling.

She gave him an indulgent look. "The night's not going to get any warmer."

Cash smiled self-consciously. "Name's Cashton."

He had a damn unusual name and thought for sure it would register with her. But if it did, she said or showed nothing that betrayed her knowledge.

As they went through the iron gate and started up the walkway to the house, she said in a very quiet voice, "I know who you are."

With that admission Cash stopped short.

She turned to him, and half of her face was bathed in the glow of moonlight, somehow softening her features so that she suddenly looked young and attractive.

"I knew who you were the first night you came into the café," she said.

"Yeah?" Cash said warily.

"Sam told me . . . when I was getting your coffee."

"Reckon that answers one of my questions," Cash said.

"Suppose it does." Lucinda smiled.

"I gotta admit, you had me questioning. The way you was lookin' at me and all."

"Well," she said mildly, "I was curious about you."

"Like a lot of folks," Cash said, twisting his mouth into a grimace. "But I still can't figger—"

Lucinda shivered and wrapped the shawl tightly around her shoulders. "It's cold," she said. "Let's go inside." Then she paused. "Unless you've gotta be somehere."

"Not tonight."

They went inside the house, and, as she had the last time, she lit the table lamps in the parlor, then immediately went into the other room to change out of her uniform.

She said from behind the door, "If you'd care for a drink, liquor's in the same place."

"You?" Cash offered.

"Why not? It'll help take off the chill."

Cash went into the kitchen. The bottle of corn whiskey had exactly the same amount as he remembered from last week. At least she wasn't much of a drinker, he thought to himself.

He brought the glasses into the parlor, setting hers on the table by the sofa and placing his own on the opposite end. Tonight he decided not to sit away from her on the rocker.

He sipped his drink, the taste of which had not improved with age over the past week. He smoked one cigarette, then another. She seemed to be taking a long time getting changed. The wait started to push his thoughts into the same direction they had gone before. With one brand-new question to be answered: if she knew who he was, that he'd spent time in prison, why the hell was she so interested? Unless she was a gold digger who maybe thought he had stashed away some of the bank loot from Hensford. But looking around at how she lived, she sure didn't look like she had any great need for money. The questions kept coming. So, then, if she could afford all this, why was she working at a crummy little café as a waitress?

None of it made any sense to him.

Soon she stepped from the room. She was in her nightwear and a robe—nothing to suggest she had something extra in mind, just comfort.

"I hope you don't mind," she said without embarrassment. "I like to relax after work."

"Don't go out much?" Cash asked her mildly.

"Some. Not a lot. I've only been in town for a short while. Plus I'm usually so tired after work that all I'm up for is a hot cup of tea and a good book."

Cash nodded and glanced at the books she had neatly shelved in the corner bookcase. He did some reading, which was the major part of his education, but he couldn't recognize any of the stuff she had lined up in there.

She seated herself on the sofa and reached for her drink. She raised the glass in a toast. Cash joined her, and they both took a sip.

She immediately wore a sour face. "This stuff is terrible."

"Tasted better myself," Cash agreed. "Don't usually drink whiskey for the taste, though."

She considered her glass briefly, then placed it on the coffee table. "That's the first drink I've taken from that bottle. And the last."

Once they were settled and comfortable, Cash decided to start asking those questions that had him scratching his head.

"I gotta be truthful, Lucinda," he said. "I don't mean to sound outta place, but none of this adds up to me."

"There's really nothing more to it than my wanting to know you," she said innocently.

"Because?" he asked, the glint of suspicion in his eyes.

Lucinda only briefly considered her answer. "I don't know. You're . . . different from most people I've known in my life. Guess in a way you represent what it was that I came looking for in Wyoming."

"An outlaw who's done time?" Cash said with a grim humor.

"No," Lucinda said immediately. Her face scrunched up as she seemed to be searching for what it was she was trying to say. Then her eyes brightened. "You're . . . an 'individual.' Someone honest with who he is."

"And you find that . . . to your likin'?" Cash said, furrowing his brow.

"I find it *interesting*," she said. "And I suppose appealing, in a way. I guess for this to make any sense to you, I should explain. Before I came to Wyoming, I had a privileged life. Pampered, I guess you could call it. My family owned land and ranches in California. And as the only girl in a family of five brothers, I wasn't protected as much as I felt suffocated. I didn't know much about the outside world until I was well into my teen years. By that time I decided I wanted to experience life on my own terms, not those that were expected of me by my family."

"You was lookin' to bust loose," Cash said with a crooked smile.

Lucinda smiled back with her straight white teeth showing, quietly amused at his straightforward way of talking.

"That's one way of saying it. One day I said good-bye to my family and went out on my own." Lucinda lowered her eyes sadly. "Only that's not the end of the story."

"Go on," Cash gently urged her.

She drew a deep breath that she held for a moment before releasing. "I met a man—in Utah. A man with a good background and fine manners. He came from a family with money too. But after we were married, I discovered that he wasn't a good person. In fact, he was a cruel, brutal man. Dominating. I stayed with him for almost eight years because I was afraid to leave. Eight years of hell, where he seemed to do everything that he could to belittle me and make my life miserable. I put up with it for those eight years only because he said he'd kill me if I ever tried to leave him. And seeing the way he could get, I didn't doubt he would. But the day finally came . . ." Her words drifted off.

Listening to that, Cash felt a rush of sympathy for Lucinda. He could see how difficult this was for her, so he told her she didn't have to say any more. But she upraised a hand in a gesture telling him it was all right, and she took a moment to compose herself.

She continued. "For a couple of years I moved around a lot. Always afraid that he'd find me. The thing is, I don't even know if he ever really came looking."

"You never thought of goin' back to your family?" Cash asked.

Lucinda regarded him with a frown. "No, of course not. They'd never understand. A woman doesn't just up and leave her man. Besides, I wouldn't have put it past my brothers to come gunning for Charles."

"Sounds to me like it wouldn't be no loss if'n they did," Cash offered.

Lucinda didn't respond to that. She looked pensive. "But for all those years I lived with a hypocrisy that no one else saw but me. A man who could be charming to a fault with others but cold and cruel to me. When it came to money, he gave me a fine life, but I was just another possession. One that he could kick around like a pair of old shoes."

They sat quietly for a few minutes. Then Cash got up to pour himself another drink, and when he came back into the parlor, Lucinda had more to tell.

"The one good thing that came out of those years I was away from Charles was that I needed to find a job. What I discovered about myself was that I enjoyed working. That was something I'd never had to do before. First at home, then with my husband. I never learned how to take care of myself. So, after my father died and I came into some money, I wasn't about to stop working. That explains how I came by this house and why I work as a waitress."

"Reckon it does," Cash said. "But why waitressin'?"

"Why not? It's honest work, and I get to meet interesting people." She gave Cash a sideways look and a gentle smile.

"Figger people 'round here would think it somewhat peculiar. Workin' that kinda job and livin' alone in this big house? Might get 'em to thinkin' . . ." Cash didn't finish, but the glance Lucinda tossed his way told him she knew what he was hinting at.

"People will think what they want. I can't let that bother me," she said, unconcerned. "But I haven't really found that here. Well . . . maybe some in the beginning. Of course I did find out that this house has a history. But now I do my job, and no one troubles me." She sighed. "Maybe how I live is elaborate—some might even call it eccentric—but I was taught that money is for spending. And I wanted to hold on to something I was used to."

Cash scratched the nape of his neck. "Reckon that answers most everythin'. 'Ceptin' how I come into this."

She told him. "I heard about you almost from the first day I arrived in Wyatt City. You might find this difficult to believe, but some of the people here admire you. Not for what you did, of course. But because you took your punishment like a man. At first I thought it a strange kind of respect."

Cash was bitterly amused. "Yeah. Respected so much I couldn't get a job cleanin' barns after I got out."

"I know. I heard all the talk at the café. And the more I heard, the more I learned about you. The type of man you were. How you'd had it hard growing up and had to play dirty even to get the crumbs a man like my husband would throw to a dog before sharing with someone like you." She hesitated for a time; then her words came very softly. "Maybe I also understood because you were in prison. Because in my own way I knew what that was like. Prisons don't always come with bars."

It was right pretty talk. But to Cash, none of what Lucinda was saying cleared up anything. In fact, he was starting to feel a strange resentment toward her. And he didn't want to feel that. He was beginning to like this gal. He figured that because of her open friendliness she liked him too. But now he was starting to wonder how genuine her feelings really were, if they were based more on *what* he was than *who* he was. He remembered the way it was with Ethan's friends, who thought that his outlaw reputation was something to admire, that being a criminal made him some sort of hero. That was not the kind of liking Cash wanted, especially not from a woman. Especially not from *this* woman.

Without saying a word, Cash stood up to leave. As he saw it, better to end things now, before there were hard feelings.

He watched the smile fade from Lucinda's lips.

"I said something wrong?" she said quietly, her voice uncertain.

"Ain't sure," Cash said as gently as he could. "Got a lot goin' on in my life right now. And to be truthful . . . I don't know if I'm comfortable with any of what you're tellin' me."

"About . . . how I feel?"

"Yeah," Cash replied. Without intending to, he added, "Mebbe . . . how we both feel."

She started to speak, but Cash stopped her. He didn't know the proper words to say. Maybe he was wrong about her, her real intentions. He'd never gotten too close to many women to figure out how they were thinking. But now it just seemed wrong to him. Another time and things might have been different. But there was just too much tugging at him right now.

And there was more. A truth he had been fighting back that suddenly came rushing at him like a whirlwind.

He couldn't let this girl or anyone else get close to him.

Because he didn't know if he had a future past Wednesday.

Chapter Seven

Cash went home to try to get some shut-eye, and when he found that sleep was as difficult as it had always been, he sat up for a spell with some coffee, tried to read but couldn't seem to concentrate, then finally went for an early walk through town. He enjoyed the fresh morning air that drifted across the valley from off the distant mountains, and most especially he appreciated the solitude that preceded the breaking of dawn. He was still feeling pretty confused about the night before. He'd been hoping for some straight answers to the mystery of why Lucinda had been so uncommonly forthright with her apparent interest in him, but she was still talking in riddles. In fact, he'd begun to question the truth behind that story she'd given him. It was evident she'd come from a privileged background and had money. But Cash wasn't quite so sure about her marriage and the rest.

The funny thing was, all that aside, she seemed to have found herself a permanent spot in his thoughts. And Cash was wondering if that little part of his brain knew something the rest of him didn't.

But what was the use? With what he would soon set out to do, he had to keep his head clear, and getting involved with a woman now would only add a complication he sure didn't need.

Later, Cash dropped by Doc Pedersen's office for a check on Ma's condition. The doctor really started to lay on the guilt about Cash's not having gone out to see her yet. Cash finally had to say to him that if Ma remained asleep, he couldn't see the point of the long ride out to Stafford. Besides which, he added, he didn't even own a horse. Ma was being cared for. There was nothing his being there could do for her. Cash spoke those words harshly, but it was mostly the truth.

Doc Pedersen finally just sighed and shrugged. But he did say that the hospital would be needing more money. That was one thing. Then he also mentioned that the doctors there had suggested bringing in some kind of specialist from Boston. Doc Pedersen felt it was a good idea—that, while there were no guarantees, it might be of some help in determining the long-term effects of Ma's illness. Much as Cash wanted to tell him just to have the hospital send for this special doctor, he couldn't appear too agreeable. That was a lot of money Pedersen was talking about. Money he knew Cash didn't have handy. So Cash simply told him that he had been working on a deal with some business owners in Laramie and that if it came though like he was expecting, he should have some cash by the beginning of the next week.

Cash didn't know if the doctor believed him. He probably was as doubtful about that as he seemed to be about everything Cash had been telling him. Cash was just glad the doc didn't start to ask questions—like wanting to know what sort of a business deal.

He left Doc Pedersen's office and started back for home. He didn't get far when a fancy two-horse, four-seat carriage pulled up on the road alongside the boardwalk. He looked over to see Chick McGraw holding the reins and a grinning and sharply dressed, derby-donning Steve Reno sitting beside him.

"Got your day planned?" Steve asked.

Cash walked over to the carriage. He then noticed the huge bulk of Slug Fletcher occupying the backseat.

"Not really," he replied, somewhat hesitantly.

"Thought we'd take a little ride into the country," Steve said. He leaned forward in his seat and gazed out from under the fringed canopy into the clear skies. "Beautiful day for it."

Cash knew instantly that what Reno had in mind was no simple country ride. He had a specific destination, and Cash didn't have to guess where that was.

He gave a short nod, though privately wishing he was anyplace else in the world, and started to climb in back, next to Slug. Slug grunted over his cigar and shifted his ample girth to make some room. Then off they rode down the main street of Wyatt City, looking to the citizens out and about like respectable gentlemen on a morning business trip.

Respectable gentlemen . . . going to check on the place Steve had chosen for their hideout.

It was a quiet ride, and Cash was glad for that at least, as he wasn't much in the mood for talk. Once they got near the location of the hideout, Steve, Slug, and Cash climbed out, leaving Chick to watch the buggy while they went on foot along the tricky terrain and down through the dense underbrush that led to the cabin.

Even as he struggled through this short journey, Cash grudgingly had to hand it to Steve. The place he'd picked for the gang to lay low after the holdup was perfect. A long-deserted cabin nestled among a thick cluster of trees and a camouflage of shrubbery, a swiftly running stream nearby. While the cabin itself offered nothing by way of comforts, it was so well hidden that even an experienced tracker would have a difficult time finding his way there. Steve had done his homework well.

He told Cash to go inside and look around. The cabin was already stocked with canned grub and other essentials to see the men through their wait, which Steve had guaranteed wouldn't be for more than a few days.

Cash didn't much care for the thought of spending even a few *hours* cooped up with Slug and the Indian, Andy Chelsea. But he had no choice. It was part of the plan. As Steve had explained, it would take that time for the Beckerman detective to make his false identification.

After they rode back into town, Steve suggested that they stop in at Dead Eye Molly's for a few drinks. Andy Chelsea was there waiting for them, sipping a cup of coffee and eyeing the men vacantly as they entered. There was food and lots of liquor, which Steve pulled out a big wad of bills to pay for. Molly served them personally and came by often to see if they needed anything. She was always accommodating whenever she saw money generously spread around. On the other hand, she got annoying as she kept repeating how good it was to see "the boys" together again. Cash wondered how happy she would be if she found out she wouldn't be profiting from their upcoming job. Molly never liked to be kept out of anything that could make her a few dollars.

Andy Chelsea was a new addition. He regarded Molly with the cold stare and icy silence he presented to everyone. But as long as the dollars kept slapping into her hand, Molly stayed happy and treated Andy with the same cloying familiarity she did each of "the boys."

Afterward Steve announced that he had one more treat in store. They would be attending a bare-knuckle bout that was to be held that evening in a hall just outside of town. Cash knew about the fight; it had been promoted for weeks as a major event in Wyatt City, but he'd given it little thought, since he had more important concerns running through his head.

He didn't know much about boxing and wasn't particularly keen on going, but Steve was insistent and, as always, persuasive, so after their afternoon at Dead Eye Molly's they each—except for the Indian, who preferred to stay behind—climbed into the buggy and drove the few miles to the community hall.

The place was packed when they got there. It looked as if men from all over Wyoming had come to see the action. The benches were occupied by boisterous, eager spectators, all ready to see blood spilled. The air inside the hall was hot and cloudy with mingled cigar and cigarette smoke. Steve had his own cigar clamped between his teeth. He walked his small group to benches he'd reserved in the front row. He occasionally stopped along the way to cheerfully acknowledge a greeting from an acquaintance. A lot of people seemed to know Steve Reno, and he reveled in all the attention.

After the men were seated, with Cash on Steve's right and Slug and Chick sitting to his left, Steve turned to Cash and said, loudly enough to be heard over the noise of the crowd, "Y'want some action, compadre? I can stake you to a hundred. Mace Keller'll take down Siegel by the third round."

Steve seemed pretty confident of the outcome, so Cash thought *What the hell*, and accepted his offer. There was no question he could use the money. Steve told Chick to go place the bet with some guy in the hall who was handling the action. He then settled back and sucked on his cigar.

His eyes were focused straight ahead on the ring when he said, "Heard you were up to see your brother."

Hell, Cash thought. *Nothing gets by this guy.*

"Yeah," he acknowledged.

"He doin' okay?" Steve asked offhandedly.

"He's doin' okay," Cash said back to him.

Steve nudged him with his elbow. "See, what'd I tell you? My partners are men of their word."

The spectators fell quiet as some guy stepped into the center of the ring to introduce the referee, then the two fighters. The crowd mostly cheered for Mace Keller and booed at his opponent, Larry Siegel, who, at least to the untrained eye, looked definitely outmatched.

Cash glanced sideways past Steve to Slug Fletcher. His face was set and impassive. But Cash noticed that his huge hands were tightly clenched and held firmly against his thighs. He wondered whether Slug was thinking about his own short-lived career as a fighter.

The first round came and went without much action. The two fighters kept their distance, circling, jabbing, connecting with only a few ineffective blows. The audience started to boo and hiss to show their disapproval at the slow action.

In round two, the fighters started slugging. It was obvious that the kid named Mace Keller had the advantage. Twice he knocked Larry Siegel to the ground, and each time he had to be pulled back by the referee as he charged in for more. Siegel looked dazed both times he unsteadily got back to his feet.

By the middle of the third round, Mace Keller was pummeling his opponent, finally landing a powerful fist against Siegel's jaw that sent him hurtling over the ropes and landing damn near the feet of the front-row spectators. Cash got his first good look at Siegel and saw that his face looked like a side of raw beef. The audience jumped to its feet and started hollering and cheering—

while Steve simply turned to Cash with a smug, satisfied look on his face.

"Just got myself five hundred bucks, compadre. Easiest money I ever made."

His comment hit Cash with almost the same force as Mace Keller's winning blow. He forgot about the fight and even the fast hundred he'd just made. He really hadn't thought about it before . . . but it now occurred to him that Steve Reno was playing fast and loose with his money. His fancy hotel, wild spending, and now betting on fights. Cash knew he'd been paid some up-front money for the job they were getting ready to pull. But the way Steve was throwing money around, Cash couldn't help thinking that what he'd handed him as an "advance" was just chicken feed. He was starting to grow mighty curious about just how much money was actually involved in this deal—and how much Slug, Chick, Andy Chelsea, and he would actually see. Might just amount to more chicken feed compared to what Steve could be hauling in. And the thing was . . . how would any of them know? Steve was the one doling out the dollars.

After the winnings had been collected and Steve went over to congratulate his "benefactor," he invited some people back to his hotel for a little celebration. Cash didn't want to go, but it was never easy to say no to Steve Reno.

Steve was a generous host, ordering food and bottles of champagne from the dining room. He even had some saloon girls come up to entertain for the party. Cash wasn't surprised not to see Andy Chelsea there, but Slug was present, sitting morosely by himself off in a corner. Cash wasn't exactly enjoying himself, either, despite Steve's efforts to corral him with one of the saloon gals. But he simply wasn't in the mood.

What surprised him most was how Steve could be so at ease and entertaining this lavishly when in less than forty-eight hours they were going to be pulling off a stagecoach robbery sure to go down in Wyoming history. A robbery where each of the participants knew beforehand that men would be killed.

But it was apparent that none of this bothered Steve Reno,

who mingled among his guests, laughing and joking, looking as if he didn't have a care in the world.

Steve finally ushered Cash into the quiet area of his bedroom, closing the door behind them. He looked disappointed.

"You don't seem to be enjoyin' yourself, compadre," he said.

Cash was only half-truthful. "Reckon I'm thinkin' 'bout Wednesday."

Steve started to build a cigarette, his slender fingers working with smooth precision.

"Havin' doubts?"

"Some," Cash admitted.

Steve lit a match against the carved wood of the bedpost and inhaled deeply from his cigarette. As he blew out a ring of smoke, he said, "Not a good time to be gettin' second thoughts."

Cash spoke his concern. "Still ain't comfortable with the killin'."

Steve spoke plainly. "That's the way it's gotta be. But if'n it'll make you feel a little better, I heard from my partners, and they've got everything set on their end. Meanin' that we walk away from this clear—and rich. There's nothin' for us to worry 'bout—if each of us follows the plan."

"What 'bout the money?" Cash asked, to get his mind off what he didn't want to further contemplate.

Steve squinted deviously. "Money's already here. But my partners' instructions are, nobody gets paid till the job is done."

Nobody but Steve Reno, Cash thought sourly. And Steve's admission about the pay answered a lot about how he was managing to live with such extravagance. It wasn't from the so-called upfront money he'd gotten. He'd already been digging into the whole payload. Either his partners' instructions didn't apply to him, or, as Cash was already starting to suspect, he was helping himself to his own share and maybe even skimming a bit from what was coming to the others.

The look on Steve's face suddenly shifted into an expression that almost looked as if he were daring Cash to challenge him on what he figured he suspected. He knew Cash wasn't as dumb as the others, that his old partner could see how he was spending money hand over fist. Money that surely didn't come from the bank account of a man just let out of prison. He just wanted to see if or how far Cash would pursue it.

Cash *wasn't* dumb. Only there was nothing he could say. He knew he wasn't only risking his share of the money but likely his life if he even hinted that Steve was cheating them.

Steve spoke calmly, though his cold blue eyes were piercing. "Trust me, Cash. In just a few days you're gonna have more money than you ever saw before."

Cash hoped he was right. But suddenly he needed a lot more convincing.

Steve went back to his party. Cash stayed in the peace and quiet of the bedroom for a spell and tried to think things out. Sure, he wanted to trust Steve. He was a friend, a guy Cash grew up with. Hell, Steve was the fella he robbed his first bank with.

He wanted to trust Steve Reno.

He just wasn't sure that he could.

Chapter Eight

Cash awoke around sunrise on Wednesday with the strange realization that he hadn't dreamed since he'd gotten out of Bennetsville. Kind of an odd thought, but most of what was going through his brain of late was not quite ordinary. What he remembered most about the dreams he'd had in prison was they always seemed to point to a happy and even prosperous future once he got his release.

Well, prosperous . . . maybe, but by today's end he wasn't certain how happy his future was going to be.

He also awoke in a foul mood. Angry, resentful at the direction his life had taken. The odd thing was that he wanted to maintain the bad mood. He'd need it to see him through the next several hours.

He got out of bed, pumped some cold water into a basin, splashed it onto his face, and rubbed his skin dry with a towel. He didn't bother to shave. He got into his clothes and stepped outside for the short walk to the livery stable, where the horse paid and provided for by Steve's partners, acting through an agent, had been housed. Each of the men in Steve's outfit had mounts stabled in different parts of town so that no one could get suspicious seeing them all ride out from the same spot together.

Cash gave a check of his horse. He looked to be a good, sturdy animal. He got him saddled and then mounted.

It was early enough that there were hardly any citizens up and around to see him ride out of Wyatt. He rode at a steady pace to the hideout where they would all be gathering.

It was about an hour's ride. Since Cash had already been out

there, he found the place without much difficulty, but for someone not familiar with the cabin's whereabouts or the difficult terrain leading to it, it would be the devil to find. There was a very
narrow trail that cut through the trees and overgrowth, which,
with careful navigation, Cash led his horse through.

Slug Fletcher and Chick McGraw were already at the cabin. Not
even 8:00 A.M. and Cash noticed that Slug was taking big swigs
from a bottle of whiskey. Steve was always generous with the
liquor, but he'd made it known that today he wanted each of his
men to be sober and clearheaded. Of course not even Steve was going to stop Slug from having a few belts. It wouldn't matter in any
case, since Slug could drink quarts of whiskey and never show it.

Cash made a quick study of Steve. He looked calm and relaxed. But knowing him as well as Cash thought he did, he could
recognize a telltale sign of Steve's own tenseness. He was a com-
pulsive hair-comber, vain about his personal grooming. But today he was running his little ivory pocket comb through his hair
about once every couple of minutes.

As much as Cash wasn't eager to get on with the job, he could
scarcely tolerate the long waiting. The stagecoach wouldn't be
coming through until eleven, and that was still a few hours away.
Slug drank, ate a little food, and smoked cigars. The rest of the
group had coffee and rolled cigarettes.

Each had time to reflect on his own thoughts, and Cash passed
the time by guessing what was going through the heads of the
others. Slug Fletcher was the easiest to figure out. He was a brute,
a creature of pure instinct and survival who, it was doubtful, ever
gave a moment to introspective thought. Chick McGraw was the
only one of the men besides Slug who had never served time in
prison, so it didn't surprise Cash that, while he desperately tried to
conceal it, he looked nervous and fidgety sitting out his wait.

As for Cash, he had just one thought running through his brain.
Something he'd fought to keep from thinking about since the beginning. But now, with time growing short, he stopped fighting and
surrendered to that concern.

If something did go wrong today, what would become of Ma
and his brother?

He didn't want to consider that possibility and tried to push it from his mind, focusing instead on how the money would make things better. Even if Ma didn't get well, at least he could see to it that she was kept comfortable in the right facility. Maybe he could use some of the money to help set Ethan straight after he got out of prison. A toss of the coin would determine the outcome. Heads: security and possibly a promising future. Tails: Ma would become a charity case, and Ethan might grow more embittered than he already was and likely follow in the path of Steve Reno.

But those were thoughts Cash knew he couldn't contend with now.

It could all be fixed right, he silently argued . . . if everything went according to plan.

Andy Chelsea sauntered in about an hour before they were set to go. He wore no expression under his hooded eyes as he took long looks at each of the men. He looked extra hard at the half-empty bottle of whiskey that Slug had been drinking from, and then he went to the coffeepot and poured himself a cup.

With each man now present, Steve walked over to some saddle-bags lying on the floor and brought them to the table. He opened them and pulled out gun belts and five shiny new Colt revolvers. He almost made a ceremony of handing out the belts and guns. Each of the .44s was loaded to capacity. A total of thirty rounds of ammunition. More than they could ever hope to use.

At least Cash was hoping.

He noticed that Steve had a fancier gun than the rest of them. His was a Colt .45, silver-mounted, pearl handle.

Come ten thirty, the men were ready. Steve seemed to be taking a particular interest in Cash as he strapped on his gun belt. Cash finally met his eyes with a steady gaze and nodded. Steve nodded back, and Cash guessed he'd convinced him that he was going to see this through. With his rotten mood still propelling him forward, Cash almost had himself convinced.

Steve, Slug, Andy Chelsea, and Cash rode southwest, out to a stretch of clearing called Taylor's Pass, which was a seldom-used route about three miles from where the main road that led into

Wyatt City forked. Taylor's Pass was the road the Wells Fargo stagecoach would be traveling. Chick McGraw had left earlier in the wagon to get it into place before the others arrived and was going to park it out of sight not far from where the outlaws would be stopping the stage.

It was a cool morning, befitting late September, but the skies were wide and clear. The group positioned themselves on the grassy incline of a hill, barricaded on their right by a thicket of trees and shrubbery that would prevent them from being spotted by either the driver or shotgun messenger as they wheeled through.

Shortly the Wells Fargo Overland came rumbling along the trail, not at any great speed, since it was to appear as if it carried no special cargo besides passengers. Steve and his bunch sat atop their horses at the ready. Though all of the men, except the Indian, wore wide-brimmed Stetsons that would shade their eyes, none bothered to cover the lower part of his face with a drawn-up kerchief, since only one witness would be left alive—the Beckerman detective whom Steve's decision alone would spare.

Just as the stagecoach drew near, Steve let out a whoop and led his charge off the hilly incline down onto the trail. The driver quickly pulled in the reins and halted the team.

With guns drawn, Andy Chelsea and Cash pulled up along either side of the coach while Steve and Slug positioned themselves in front of the driver and shotgun messenger. Their Colts were trained on the two men, who were caught so unaware they didn't know how to respond.

Steve settled that decision for them. "Just raise your hands high, gentlemen," he said.

The shotgun messenger did as instructed, though his coach gun, a double-barrel shotgun, still rested across his knees.

Steve gestured to the weapon. "Be smart if you tossed that aside," he said politely.

The man was slow in obliging, afraid that any move on his part would earn him a bullet.

"Go on," Steve prodded. "Know you'd probably like to make a

name for yourself with Wells Fargo, but havin' *hero* engraved on your tombstone ain't much reward."

"If I reach for it . . . you gonna shoot me?" the shotgun messenger said nervously.

Steve was deliberately toying with him. "Tell you what. Do it real slow and easy, and we'll see what I got a mind to do."

"Got a family, mister," the man said with quick emphasis as he carefully lowered both his hands toward the stock and barrels of the shotgun.

"Family man, huh? Now that *is* a shame," Steve said in a tone hinting of regret.

Cash saw Steve's eyes veer toward Slug. Even though he knew what was coming, he averted his gaze from the front of the stage. Then he heard the gunshot, followed by a groan, followed by the soft thump of a body hitting the ground.

While Slug kept the now-terrified driver covered, Steve brought his mount over to where Cash was. He pointed to the luggage compartment on the roof of the coach. Protective canvas was stretched over several square-shaped protrusions that might have been mistaken for luggage. But the outlaws knew the true cargo.

A second later there was another single gunshot that echoed through the clearing. Slug had taken care of the driver.

Steve didn't even turn around. He climbed off his horse and opened the door of the coach, gesturing to those inside to get out with a waving motion of his Colt. The passengers began exiting. From where Cash was seated atop his horse, he had seen the two well-dressed men who were obviously the Beckerman detectives sitting across from each other. What Cash did not notice—what neither he nor anyone else, surely, expected—was a third passenger. A young, frightened girl barely out of her teens, dressed in a smart traveling suit and high-crowned hat, who followed the detectives out.

Steve's expression confirmed that her presence was as much a surprise to him as it was to Cash.

He said brusquely to the agents, "Who's the girl?"

"A passenger at the station," one of the men answered uncomfortably. "The stationmaster asked us to let her ride along.

She—she has an urgent family matter to attend to in Wyatt. Said she couldn't wait for the next stage." He looked at Steve and tried to justify the complication. "We weren't counting on this . . . but we couldn't very well say no without . . ." He stopped himself from speaking further.

"No," Steve said slowly. "Reckon you couldn't."

Cash listened and felt a chill rush up his spine. He fixed his eyes on Steve and waited to see what he would do. *No witnesses,* Cash kept remembering. There weren't to be any, except for the one Beckerman agent. The gang hadn't even hid their faces because of this, and Cash now saw how the girl kept scouting her pleading eyes over Steve and himself. She could identify them in an instant, and her recognition would be completely at odds with the false identification that was to be made by the surviving detective.

Cash could see Steve pondering the situation. He looked angry, his face taut and his eyes narrowed into slits. The solution was obvious, but even for a rattler like Steve Reno it was not an easy decision to make. Maybe it was in his frustration that he suddenly aimed his revolver at the older of the two detectives and fired a single shot. The girl screamed. The other man looked stunned, since to his understanding the killing of one of them was not part of the arrangement.

Steve steadied him. "Relax, you're gonna live."

Then he looked at the girl. He lowered and slowly shook his head and holstered his Colt.

Both Andy Chelsea and Slug had come around to join Steve and Cash. The next few moments were brittle.

Steve said tightly, "This ain't the way it was supposed to be."

Slug spoke in his thin, raspy voice. "Mebbe not. But we gotta finish this the way we're s'posed to."

Steve unglued his stare from the girl and slowly turned his head toward Slug. Cold as he was, Steve couldn't bring himself to personally murder an innocent young girl. But Slug was an entirely different animal. He could do it easily, without blinking an eye.

By now Chick McGraw was pulling up in the wagon.

"Slug, take her into those trees," Steve instructed impatiently, pointing to a general area in the woods. "The rest of us will start unloading these boxes."

Cash turned to Chick. The look on his face was uncomprehending. Then he glanced at Andy Chelsea. His immobile expression revealed nothing. He couldn't look at the girl anymore. The poor creature was so numb with fear that she put up virtually no resistance once Slug got down from his horse and walked with her into the bush. Cash looked at Steve and gave him a hard stare. Then Steve turned to the detective, who could hardly stop himself from trembling.

"I oughta plug you," Steve said. "You knew the plan."

"It wouldn'ta looked right if we hadn't brought her," the detective anxiously tried to explain. "We couldn't afford no suspicion."

Steve nodded. "Yeah. Well, just you be rememberin', her blood is on *your* hands." He looked with intent at the dead agent lying on the ground.

"You owe me," Steve then said. "I was given orders to kill one of you. I made my choice. You got lucky. Remember that when you get into Wyatt. You mess up, amigo, and I'll find you."

The detective swallowed hard and gave his head a vigorous nod.

Steve gestured to the road with his gun. "You got a long walk into town. Get movin'."

Once he was far off down the trail, Steve gave the others a hand with the last heavy box of gold.

"I'm fightin' every urge not to give it to him in the back," he said through gritted teeth, his eyes frequently shifting to the departing figure.

Cash spoke up to release what he was feeling. "Lettin' him live and killin' that girl is a poor exchange."

Steve looked at him coldly. "She's the one that'll hang you," was all he said.

Before the men loaded that last box onto the wagon, Steve had them lay it on the ground. Then he motioned for everyone to step aside while he aimed his Colt at the lock and fired.

The lock blew open, and Steve lifted the lid. The gang bent in to look and saw neatly stacked bars of gold filling the inside.

"Hadda make sure we got the right cargo," Steve said, agitated. "Damn well don't know who I can trust now."

Cash thought it ironic to hear Steve Reno talking about trust.

They closed the lid and lifted the box onto the wagon with the others. Then the four men waited—for the gunshot from the woods. Only it didn't come. But soon Slug did. Alone.

No one had to ask. Slug was massaging his big, meaty hands. He'd taken care of the girl all right—but in his own brute, primitive manner.

The men all were silent. The air surrounding them was quiet, motionless, except for a sudden, faint whisper of wind rustling through the leafy trees where somewhere a girl's body lay. A girl who had innocently boarded the stage that morning, never realizing she'd not live to reach her destination. Dead men lay sprawled on the ground. Cash felt a little queasy and tried his damndest not to let it show. Even knowing that this had been planned as the outcome, the realization hit him harder than expected as his eyes surveyed the carnage.

Our handiwork, Cash thought with a deep swallow. He'd never fired a shot, but he was as guilty as Steve, Slug, and the others. Even if he went to trial and a jury acquitted him, Cash understood he would live with his own blame for the rest of his days. Suddenly the money and all that he had hoped it would do seemed worthless. How could Cash feel proud about helping Ma and his brother when he knew that the dollars he'd earned had cost people—innocent people—their lives?

Steve walked up beside him. "We'd better ride," he said curtly.

Cash nodded glumly and started for his horse.

Then Steve's voice came from behind him. "Compadre?"

Cash halted, then turned around.

And looked straight at the .45 Colt that his friend now had trained on him.

Steve's expression was dead flat as he pulled the trigger.

Chapter Nine

Another dreamless sleep.

. . . And when Cash awoke, it was to a searing pain in his shoulder, close to his chest. He was lying on the cool ground under a now-warming sun. It took him a while to collect his thoughts, but gradually he remembered where he was . . . and because of the warmth that blanketed his body, he figured that it had to be somewhere around midafternoon. He turned his head and saw the stagecoach still sitting where it had been stopped.

Cash knew instantly that he had been left for dead. He remembered that it had been Steve who'd shot him, and the pain of that knowledge hurt almost as badly as the hole in his shoulder. Steve must have thought he'd killed him with that single bullet; otherwise he would have finished the job.

But Cash wasn't dead. Not yet anyhow.

He moved his hand to where his shoulder hurt, and when he pulled it away, he saw that his fingers were covered in blood. He was weak and dizzy and almost didn't dare try to move for fear of blacking out again. But he had to. He was lucky in that the trail the stage had taken was remote and hardly journeyed—planned that way out of necessity. No one had yet come upon the massacre. He had to get away before someone did show up.

He struggled to his feet, then steadied himself once he had fully risen, clutching his shoulder against the pain and to staunch the flow of blood.

His brain was flooded with questions, but he knew his first priority was to find safety and somehow get the bullet removed. All the horses were gone, including the team that had drawn the stagecoach. Steve had taken all precautions. Cash doubted he could make it far, but he would have to try.

Cash got himself another shock when his eyes fell upon a fourth body lying in the dirt. He hadn't been the only victim of Steve Reno's betrayal. Chick McGraw was facedown with a bullet hole in his back. Cash went over to check him. He was dead and already cold. His recently fired Colt was clutched in his hand.

Cash got a queer, unsettling feeling then. He removed the Colt from his holster and flipped open the cylinder. Two shots had been discharged. He emptied the spent cartridges and considered the possibility that maybe there never were any skinners to take the blame for the robbery. That maybe it was in Steve's plan all along to frame Chick and himself.

That made matters urgent. Chick no longer had any worries. But Cash had to decide where to try to get. He thought he could recall where the hideout was—not too far, if his addled brain was remembering correctly. But even if he could crawl there, that was the one place he couldn't go. Steve thought he was dead. As long as Cash was breathing, he would have to stay clear of him and let him go on thinking that he was deceased. Otherwise his life wouldn't be worth a Confederate dollar.

Cash had no choice. He would have to start walking. Keep on for as long as he was able.

He walked . . . and rested. And walked some more. He was pushing himself forward with every ounce of strength he had left to him. And it wasn't just physical strength. Cash called upon all his will. A will strengthened by his resolve that Ma never discover that her son's body had been found near the site of a violent crime, as one of the suspected perpetrators.

Soon he came to the stream in the woods that flowed some distance along past the gang's hideout. His throat was parched, so he carefully lowered himself onto his belly and dipped his head into the cool water and drank. When he'd had his fill, he sat up and ripped open his shirt at the collar, tugging it down, and splashed water onto his wound to clean it. Luckily, the bleeding had slowed. But he still had to get the bullet out or risk infection.

Cash carried a small knife in his pocket. Now he had water to

cleanse it. Wishing he also had a good shot of whiskey to help
numb what was to come, he flicked opened the blade and swirled
it around in the running water of the stream. He took a moment
to inhale several deep breaths. Then as gently and carefully as he
dared, Cash pushed the sharp tip into the wound and tried to lo-
cate the bullet. He was quickly bathed in sweat, as wet as if he'd
just pulled himself whole from the waters of the stream. The pain
made him want to cry out, but he clamped his teeth together until he felt the point of the blade touch something hard and solid—
and deep inside his flesh. He was close to blacking out as he
forced his hand to keep steady and slid the blade forward still
more, to where it reached the blunt head of the bullet. Cash gin-
gerly curved the blade just a fraction and then started lightly prying at the slug. He could feel the blood start to flow again, but
despite the bleeding and an agony so intense that not even the
devil himself could have dreamed it up, he kept twisting the
blade and prying. He couldn't . . . he *wouldn't* stop. As much as
he wanted to, Cash would not withdraw the knife until the bullet
came with it.

The ordeal seemed like an eternity. Cash didn't know how long
it took—nor could he guess how much damage he might have
caused in extracting the slug—but he finally pried the bullet close
enough to the surface where he could reach his fingers into the
bloody hole and pull it out. He unclenched his jaw, which had been
locked so tightly that his back teeth should have been ground into
powder. Then he swiftly scooped up more handfuls of water that
he washed into the wound. Finally, before all his strength was
spent, he used his knife to cut off a small piece from the tail of his
shirt, dipped the cloth into the water, and pressed the material
against the hole, stuffing some of it inside, deep enough to hope-
fully halt the bleeding.

Cash knew he couldn't travel any farther. Not until he rested.
He wasn't even sure that he'd ever wake from the sleep he now
desperately needed. If his makeshift bandage didn't do its job, he
would probably bleed to death within a couple of hours. But
Cash had done all that he could. What was to be was now out of

his hands. But if he survived and could somehow regain and hold on to his strength, he would try to get himself back to Wyatt City.

He was sharply nudged awake from one of the deepest sleeps he had known in a long while. His first thought was that he was surprised to find himself still alive. . . .

But not nearly as surprised as he was to discover who was crouched before him with the barrel of a Colt revolver aimed close to his forehead.

Sheriff Garrett O'Dowd.

Cash quickly tried to collect his thoughts but dared not shift his body even an inch. Garrett looked calm, but Cash couldn't guess how steady his trigger finger was.

"Mighta known you was one of 'em," Garrett said tonelessly.

"How did you . . . ," Cash said faintly.

"Weren't hard to find, McCall," he said, anticipating the question. "Just followed the trail of blood you left behind. Pretty much leadin' from where you left the stage . . . and them bodies."

Cash noticed that Garrett's other hand held his Colt with the two empty chambers . . . and probably still smelling of gun smoke. That evidence was sure to put a noose around his neck.

"Always knew you was no good, McCall, ever since we was kids," Garrett said as he fiddled with Cash's gun. "But this time you really crossed the line."

Cash felt weak and fevered and sick in the stomach, like he wanted to throw up. His whole body seemed to be drenched in sweat. He lifted his eyes and looked through the leafy overhang of the trees that surrounded him. It had to be getting around dusk, as the skies were darkening. Cash reckoned he hadn't been asleep for long. But certainly long enough for Garrett to track him.

The sheriff looked at the shoulder wound, and Cash's eyes traveled with him. The cloth from his shirt had maybe slowed the bleeding but might not have stopped it, since the material was soaked red.

Garrett had a look on his face resembling concern. He tilted the Stetson up over his brow. "I'm gonna get you into town. Get the doc to see if he can patch you up. Then I expect you to be answerin' some questions."

Garrett helped Cash to his feet, and none too gently. Cash couldn't seem to steady himself as the sheriff led him to his horse. His head was spinning. But he still had enough of his wits about him to understand what was happening. He knew he needed a doctor, but after he was fixed up, he'd be jailed. He'd be tried—with no defense. And then . . . it was almost certain he would be convicted and hanged.

It was all too easy. Too unfair. If Cash had to die, he first had to even the score with Steve Reno. And before that, he had to know why Reno had left him for dead.

They were standing next to the horse. Cash couldn't put up a fight, so Garrett holstered his gun and slid Cash's Colt into his saddlebag.

Cash had just one slim chance to make his move.

He groaned and started to drop in a pretend faint. Garrett instinctively grabbed at his ribs with both hands to hold him up. The hand that Cash could still use came up swiftly, closed in a fist, landing under Garrett's chin. Cash hit him with as much strength as he still had in him, and the sheriff's head snapped back, and he crumpled to the ground. Cash's punch had knocked him out. Cash knelt next to the prone Garrett and used his good arm to roll him over onto his back. He took his gun from the holster. For one quick, crazy instant he considered putting a bullet into him. Cash didn't know if Garrett had come out alone, but it was he alone who had found him. So Cash figured Garrett had to be the only one who knew that he had taken part in the stagecoach robbery.

To Cash it was a hard decision. He even put the barrel close to Garrett's head, as the sheriff had done to him. But his conscience was troubled enough. He'd seen enough senseless killing for one day. And he didn't hold a grudge against Garrett. The sheriff was just doing his job. So, for better or for worse, Cash let him live. He'd have to hide out instead until he could get well enough to do anything else.

Cash retrieved his own six-shooter from the sheriff's saddlebag. He didn't want to carry an extra gun, especially one easily recognizable as the sheriff's, with its distinctive initial-inlaid polished walnut handle, and so he tossed Garrett's Colt into the underbrush.

It took some effort, but he managed to pull himself onto the sheriff's horse.

Now he only hoped he had the strength to make it into town.

Chapter Ten

Cash knew he didn't have a whole lot of options. But he did know where he had to go. It was the only place he could think of where he might be safe, at least for the time being. There was the likelihood he might not be welcome, especially in his bloodied condition and after an explanation of how he'd gotten that way. But Cash had to chance it.

He wasn't about to ride the sheriff's horse directly into Wyatt, so he let the animal loose on the outskirts of town. Cash rested a spell and checked his wound. He wasn't sure about the bleeding, but he still felt mighty weak and sicker than a dog.

He made his way into town the back way, navigating the alleys and corners where it was less likely he'd be seen. He rested periodically, since his strength was ebbing faster than perspiration in the desert. He was short of breath, and his shoulder wound was burning something awful.

He finally got to the house, which, luckily for him, was situated off the main street, away from public traffic, and was quite well protected from public view by the trees and thick greenery in the front yard.

Cash just hoped that he'd find her at home.

He carried himself up the steps and braced his body at the side of the door before he used his last ounces of strength to raise a fist to knock. It seemed like a long wait, and Cash quickly grew discouraged. He was weakening fast, and his body started to slide heavily down onto the porch.

Then the door opened. Lucinda looked out, and, turning her gaze to her right, her eyes met Cash's.

The last thing Cash remembered was the wide-eyed, open-mouthed expression that suddenly appeared on her face. . . .

The hours—days? weeks?—that followed passed as if Cash were caught in the grip of a brain fever. He would come awake, not knowing where, or even who, he was, then slip back into the blackest of unconsciousness. When he started to become more aware of his surroundings, his first visions were always of Lucinda sitting next to him, keeping him cool with compresses against his forehead and feeding him sips of water. Cash couldn't stay awake for long and always drifted back to sleep. But when he'd waken, there she'd be, still at his side.

Finally Cash was stirred awake by her gentle voice speaking his name. It was hard to leave the peaceful darkness that kept both his pain and his memories at a safe distance, but it was as if he had no choice. His eyelids fluttered open, and his first sensation was of the burning ache in his shoulder that seemed not to have eased at all.

"You're going to be all right," Lucinda said with a smile.

Cash nodded and tried to smile back.

"You had me concerned for a while," she said. "You had a high fever and a pretty bad inflammation in your shoulder. But I got the infection cleaned up, and it seems like the fever's finally broke. Your arm's still gonna be sore for a while. There looks to be quite a lot of damage."

She tactfully avoided mentioning that the "damage" looked to have been caused by a bullet.

But Cash saw no reason not to confirm what she already knew.

"Yeah," he muttered, trying to flex the fingers of his right hand, which had gone quite numb. "Hadda dig it out myself. And I ain't no doctor." Then his head rose slightly off the pillows, and he fixed her with a tight stare. "You—didn't bring no doc. . . ."

She shook her head. "No. Didn't think that'd be smart. Nursed you myself. Threw out that cloth you stuck into yourself and got you some proper bandages. Gotta change them every so often so you don't get that infection back into you."

Cash let his head settle back. "Thanks," he whispered.

"And just so you don't go worrying, no one's come around, either," she added.

"Don't mean someone won't," Cash sighed.

"I wouldn't concern myself with that. Why would anyone? No one knows . . . about us," Lucinda said timidly.

It felt good for Cash to hear her say that. With those words he felt he could trust her, take it easy until he got his strength back.

Lucinda helped lift him, and she adjusted the pillows under his head. Cash lay back, and she pulled up the covers to just below his neck.

"In case the pain gets too bad, I picked up a bottle of laudanum from the druggist."

"Reckon I could use a belt now," Cash said, exaggerating a grimace.

"Not a 'belt,' " she scolded playfully. "A spoonful. Two if you need it."

Cash winked at her. "Reckon my well-bein's in your hands."

Lucinda seemed for a moment unsure of what to say, then spoke her words softly. "Well . . . I don't know what happened. But till I do, I just want to see you get well."

Cash offered an appreciative nod. He took two spoonfuls of the laudanum, and between the swift effects of the medicine and the comfort of the bed, he was soon off to sleep.

Cash slept straight through the night, waking the following morning later than he usually would. Lucinda carried in a tray with a light breakfast of buttered toast and a little coffee, and Cash was pleased to discover that he had an appetite. He even managed to sit up on his own to eat it.

After he was done with his meal, Cash rubbed the palm of his hand along his face, which was thick with whiskers. Lucinda offered to give him a shave, and Cash was glad to accept.

Lucinda had to go out to the mercantile to pick up the shaving supplies. When she came back, she put a small towel around his shoulders and whipped up the hard cake of shaving soap into a creamy paste that she delicately applied to his cheeks and neck.

"Never had no barber do it any better," Cash said contentedly.

Lucinda's mouth crinkled in a small smile. "I haven't come to the razor yet."

She was right. Those first swipes of the straight razor felt about as comfortable as getting shaved by the rusty edge of a tin can. Cash winced but didn't complain. He understood she practically had to clear a forest from his face.

They still hadn't talked about the trouble Cash had gotten into, though Cash felt distinctly that Lucinda knew, if only by word that was sure to be out on the street. In the semi-delirious state he had been in for most of the previous days, he couldn't provide her with much of an explanation that would make sense. But now that Cash was feeling more like himself, he felt he owed her the story.

As it turned out, that wasn't necessary.

During the shave Lucinda stopped her strokes for a moment and looked as if she were debating telling Cash something. He sort of nudged his head to encourage her.

She resumed her shaving and said in an even voice, "Word's been spreading through town about what happened."

Cash didn't say anything.

She went on, still speaking calmly. "A lot of talk at the café. The sheriff has men out all over the county looking for you. He says if you aren't dead, you're likely holing up somewhere in the hills."

"Better he thinks I'm dead," Cash said. "Though it makes sense he wouldn't look for me in his own backyard. Sure he musta checked with Doc Pedersen, though, given that he knows I was wounded. Only glad you never called on him."

Lucinda waited a bit before asking, "You *were* involved in that holdup?" She was asking him directly but without accusation.

"I was," Cash answered promptly.

Her razor strokes slowed. "And those people who were killed . . . ?" she said tentatively.

Cash spoke deliberately. "I never killed no one. I won't deny that I took part in that robbery, but I never fired my gun."

"From what I've been hearing, the sheriff's got evidence."

"Yeah," Cash grunted. "*Planted* evidence. A good friend of mine took care of that." He took a deep breath that pained him in the chest. "The paper's gonna say a lot of things." He calmed myself. "Reckon what matters now is what you believe."

Lucinda took a moment before responding. "I believe *you*."

"You do?" Cash said gently, carefully.

"I . . . want to," she replied.

Cash didn't know if he was compelled by impulse or appreciation, but he reached out the arm that wasn't hurting and touched her hand. Lucinda drew close to him, and he curved his hand around her neck and lightly pulled her forward until their faces were just inches apart.

"Guess I was wrong 'bout you," he said, without elaborating.

And he kissed her. A slow, gentle kiss. He reckoned that that one kiss sealed a sort of pact between them. But as the softness of their lips came together, he also got the feeling that it might mean something more.

But any kind of romance would have to wait. His first order of business was to decide how best to handle his situation. What he was enjoying was a nice interlude, but Cash recognized he was still in a precarious position. It was important that Lucinda not change her routine. She'd have to keep on waitressing so as not to arouse any suspicions from her boss. Since she admitted to not going out much, the rest of the time she could be with him with no one thinking there was anything amiss or different about her behavior.

Thanks to Lucinda's care, Cash was up and about in a few days. She had purchased some ranch-type clothes for him at a dry-goods store, and when the clerk inquired about her odd choice of attire, Lucinda simply explained that it was for her own outdoor chores.

Cash was starting to think that Lucinda was a smart gal.

He appreciated that during his time recuperating she hadn't badgered him to tell his side of the story. But Cash knew she was curious and certainly had a right to know. After all, while it was unlikely Garrett O'Dowd and his men would ever think to check her house for their wanted criminal, she was still risking jail time if he was ever found there.

They were eating an early supper on a Friday evening when Cash finally told her about the events that had brought his bullet-injured body to her door.

She listened intently, hardly touching the food on her plate, as he laid out the details of how he'd gotten involved with a gang of outlaws to raise money to care for his sick mother, and how he had witnessed their killings of almost everyone riding on that stagecoach, then had been the victim of his "friend's" skullduggery and left for dead.

After he was done with his telling, Lucinda was silent, absorbing all that Cash had told her. She pushed her supper plate aside. Cash couldn't blame her for not having an appetite. Reliving those awful events had certainly taken away his own.

"It was wrong what you did," she finally said, her words carefully measured. "But I can see you were only trying to do what was best for your mother."

Cash appreciated her understanding, even if it sounded to him as if she might be trying to convince herself.

"Yeah," he returned. "And by tryin' to do what I thought was right, I got myself dug into a deep hole. Maybe six feet."

She gave him a long, questioning look. "Why'd he double-cross *you?*" she said with a frown. "You said he was a friend."

Cash shook his head. "I don't know. All I can figger is that Steve got greedy. With me and McGraw outta the way, there was two less shares for him to split."

Lucinda lowered her lashes as her fingers toyed with her teacup. "Guess I wasn't so wrong when I thought you needed a friend."

"Need one now," Cash agreed solemnly. "'Specially one I can trust."

Lucinda straightened in her chair, considering. She said, "Cash, why don't you tell the sheriff about this? If I believe your story, maybe he will. At least I'm sure he'd check it out."

"O'Dowd's just a county lawman," Cash argued. "From what Steve says, his partners, the men who planned the robbery, are monied and powerful and have an influence that stretches far beyond Laramie. Says they even run the Beckerman Detective Agency. No, Garrett tries to go ag'in them, he's as sure as dead."

Lucinda's face grew troubled. "Then what are you planning to do?"

Cash gave her a faint smile. "Haven't thought that far ahead yet.

But I reckon I have the advantage. Easier for someone already thought dead to hunt his quarry. They won't see that a-comin'."

Lucinda's brow furrowed. "Reno won't be so sure you're dead—if he reads the newspapers."

Cash went suddenly and completely quiet. Lucinda had brought up a fact he hadn't considered. The story of his escape from Garrett O'Dowd had been front-page news, probably read by citizens all across the state of Wyoming. There was damn little chance Steve hadn't learned of this. The article mentioned that Cash might have since died from his wound but didn't confirm it.

Steve also had to know that Cash was the one man who stood between him and the real facts behind the Wells Fargo robbery. Whether he was protected by his partners or not, Cash's being alive and knowing the truth had to be a threat to him.

"You're not safe, Cash," Lucinda said, a slight tremor in her voice. "You won't ever be . . . unless you leave Wyoming."

"That ain't the answer," Cash said wearily. "You think if Steve believes I'm alive, he won't get his partners to set those crooked Beckerman detectives after me? Won't matter where I go—they'll catch up with me. It'll look all legal, but I can promise you, they won't be bringin' me in alive to tell what I know. What's that expression: caught between a rock and a hard place?"

Cash considered another more disturbing possibility that he wouldn't share with Lucinda: if he was found first by Slug Fletcher or Andy Chelsea, neither of those two rattlers would simply kill him outright. With them he was assured of dying hard and slow.

Cash had to get his thoughts onto something else. By surrendering his thinking to the worst possible outcomes to his situation, he couldn't concentrate constructively on what he was going to do.

Unfortunately, at the moment there really didn't seem to be an answer.

And there was another concern that had to be addressed. He had to know about Ma. With him not having the money he was promised, and being laid up in bed for almost a week, he had no way of knowing what had become of her—or if she was still getting the special care she'd been given at the hospital in Stafford.

Cash was almost hesitant to find out. But it was an answer he had to know.

"Lucinda, I'm gonna ask you to do me a favor, and you gotta play this one just right."

Lucinda nodded briskly.

Cash explained. "I want you to go see Doc Pedersen and convince him you're a friend of Mrs. McCall—that's my mother. She's at the county hospital. Say nothin' 'bout me. Play ignorant if he starts askin' questions, which he most likely will. But what I need you to do is . . . find out what's happenin' with her."

"Your mother?"

"Yeah. I gotta know how she is."

Lucinda agreed. Cash then asked her if she knew Doc Pedersen. If so, he might get curious with her asking about Ma. Curious enough to start wondering if it was her who was really doing the asking. Lucinda said she had never had any dealings with him, though it was possible he may have come by the coffee shop. But he wouldn't know if Lucinda was a friend of Ma's or not. If she said she was, he'd have no reason to doubt her.

It was too late to drop by the doctor's office that night, and it certainly would look curious if she stopped by his house with such an inquiry, so Lucinda said she would go to see him first thing in the morning.

And early the next morning she did. Cash waited with heavy impatience for her to return. He tried not to dwell on it, but he had the feeling the news wouldn't be good. He just hoped it wouldn't be as bad as he feared.

He smoked cigarettes and drank some of the terrible corn whiskey while he paced the floor of the parlor, wishing he could somehow drown out the monotonous ticking of the grandfather clock, each swing of the pendulum seeming to mock his anxiety as it marked the passing seconds.

Finally he heard the front door open. Cash steadied himself as he waited for Lucinda to walk in.

She entered the room, and the somber look on her face was telling.

She struggled with words that Cash immediately knew she did not have to tell him.

"I'm so sorry, Cash," she said.

Cash stood fastened to his spot on the floor for what seemed like hours but was really just a few moments. His eyes stayed on Lucinda, but it was as if he couldn't see her anymore. His mind had gone instantly blank as the strength ebbed from his body, and he lowered himself onto the sofa and stared off numbly.

Lucinda came beside him, taking his hand in both of hers. Her gentle voice coaxed Cash back from his purgatory.

"Dr. Pedersen said she died last week. He said . . . he said she went peacefully. I—I couldn't ask him any more."

When Cash didn't respond to her words, Lucinda spoke with more emphasis, intending to comfort him. "Cash, he said there was nothing anyone could do. She was just too sick. You can't be blaming yourself."

Once Cash finally replied, the tone of his voice was muted. "Maybe not for her dying. But I sure as hell can take blame for the way she hadda live."

"Would you . . . like me to leave you alone?" she offered.

"No," he muttered. Then he asked a question that now seemed so irrelevant.

"Did he say anything . . . 'bout me?"

Lucinda shook her head. "I think he believed what I told him. That I was just someone who knew your mother."

Cash turned to face her. Her brown eyes were soft and red-rimmed, and she was looking at him with the most genuine look of compassion that anyone, outside of his mother, had ever shown him.

"No, don't go," he said again, though the words weren't really his. They came from somewhere deep inside, a long-dormant emotion that was speaking for him.

Cash gently laid a hand over both of hers, and the couple sat in the quiet of the parlor for a long time.

Chapter Eleven

Ma was dead, and Cash blamed himself for letting her die. To hell with his so-called good intentions. He'd wanted to do what was best for her, but how did he set out to accomplish that? By returning to the criminal life he swore he'd never go back to after leaving Bennetsville. Looking for quick, easy money. For most of his life he'd caused Ma heartache and grief. And now it had come to this. The only relief he could feel was that at least he couldn't bring her any more anguish.

He couldn't even afford to give his mother a decent burial. She had been taken from the hospital to a small country cemetery where she was laid under the dirt alongside paupers and other forgotten souls whose struggles and failed accomplishments had brought them to this final indignity. Cash knew how much more Ma deserved—and how not even in death was he able to provide it for her.

Ma's death also carried another regret. He'd refused to be with her during those last days in the hospital. Cash was grateful that she had died while unconscious, without pain, and maybe not even knowing what had happened to her. But . . . perhaps somehow she would have known that he was there beside her. It might have given her comfort. As it was, she'd died alone. And, as Lucinda reluctantly informed him when Cash urged her to be truthful, in the hospital charity ward.

And there was Ethan. Cash didn't know if he had been told. And in truth he didn't care. Whatever grief or guilt Ethan might be feeling if he knew Ma was gone was no longer Cash's concern.

It would have been easy for Cash to slip into self-pity. But instead the opposite happened. He became strengthened with a new sense of purpose. It was as if everything that was rotten inside of him was pushing forward to give vent. As much as he was to blame for failing Ma, there was someone else who had to share responsibility. Had he not betrayed Cash with a bullet . . . things might have turned out different. Cash would never know for sure, of course, but there always may have been that chance.

But he'd taken that chance away—and now Cash owed him.

He didn't know how or when the time would come, but Cash McCall made a vow right then and there that Steve Reno would pay with his life for what he'd done.

Naturally Cash never told Lucinda what he was aiming to do. She was worried enough as it was. She wasn't concerned for her safety—only his. She still thought Cash's best plan was to sneak away one night and leave Wyoming, possibly head north, maybe into Canada, where neither Steve Reno nor his partners or even the Beckerman detectives had any influence. She was right. That probably was the smart decision. But she couldn't know how determined Cash had become to even the score with The Whiskey Kid.

Still, he would have to wait. He couldn't risk going out onto the streets, since his face was known in Wyatt City—especially now. In the event he *was* alive, a reward of five thousand dollars from Wells Fargo had been posted for his capture, accompanied by a rather good etching of Cash McCall's likeness that he got a look at when Lucinda snatched one of the posters. Cash was almost flattered to be regarded so highly.

That was when he learned he really could trust Lucinda. Even with all the money she seemed to have, five thousand dollars was a might handsome sum for easy work. All she had to do was walk into the sheriff's office on any given day and tell Garrett that Cash McCall was hiding out at her house. Of course that could make her an accessory, but Cash was sure Garrett would be so pleased to have him in jail that he'd dismiss any wrongdoing on her part. Yet even when Cash would joke with Lucinda about freeing herself of his burden, at the same time adding nicely to her wealth, she'd look upset and scold him even for suggesting such a thing.

At least in one regard Cash could count himself lucky.

In an odd yet natural way Cash could even admit to falling a bit in love with this gal whose motives he still couldn't completely figure out. He often had to wonder if even she knew what they were.

Outside of a permanent twinge in his shoulder and somewhat limited use of his arm and hand, Cash had pretty much made a full recovery. Though as the days passed, he started to get antsy. He felt imprisoned, as if he was back in his cell at Bennetsville. The house was large and comfortable, but out of necessity he was still confined. He could only risk a few minutes of outdoor air late at night when he could be sure the streets were empty, and then he would walk out in the front yard among the trees and the outer greenery, occasionally with Lucinda but most often alone so that he could clear his head and think. Hiding out at Lucinda's had been a smart idea in the beginning, but now that he was ambulatory and itching to get out, it was probably the worst place he could be. All of Wyatt City seemed to be closing in around him.

Lucinda brought Cash the Wyatt City *Register* daily, and while the articles had grown shorter, since there simply wasn't anything new to report, items continued to appear detailing the sheriff's search for the fugitive. Garrett still wouldn't confirm that Cash was dead, simply because no body had been found. And Garrett was proving himself a stubborn cuss. He wanted Cash bad, maybe because a seriously injured and unarmed man had managed to knock him down and escape in the process, making him look like a fool. He had something to prove now. To the town, but mostly to himself.

It was mid-October. The approach of night was coming earlier now. Soon snow would be on the ground. Cash doubted he could stay cooped up through the long winter season. But Lucinda believed that if his corpse hadn't been found by winter, the sheriff and his men would give up their search and declare Cash McCall dead. Once that was announced, come spring they could plan their move to Canada.

We, she had said. *Our* move.

If Cash had been planning to leave Wyoming, he had to confess that he hadn't counted on bringing Lucinda along. Not that he didn't want her companionship, but he was always going to be looking over his shoulder, and what kind of life was that for her? Her argument, and a right practical one, was that they would need money to make a new start—and *she* had money.

Cash considered that maybe they would make such a move. But not until he first saw Steve Reno dead. That was his priority, and nothing—neither love nor practicality—was going to change it.

On this day, a Tuesday, Lucinda had gone out to the market to pick up groceries for supper. She was slow in returning, and only for an instant did Cash consider that she might have made that stopover at the sheriff's office, which he had kidded her about. Of course his more sensible side reminded him that that was foolish thinking. Being locked indoors for so long often got his thoughts moving in foolish directions.

She finally got home at around four o'clock. She had bought some meat and vegetables along with a bottle of good whiskey that Cash had asked her to bring. He sat with her at the kitchen table, having a relaxing belt, while she prepared the meal.

She seemed to be in a quiet mood, and Cash wondered if something might be bothering her. Finally, just to make some conversation, he said, "Reckon this ain't been much fun for you."

She didn't answer. She just turned her head toward him slightly and smiled wanly.

"You ain't usually this quiet, Lucinda," Cash said.

Still no reply.

"Look," he said, "why don't you go out tonight? I read in the paper there's a show playin' down at the Palace. When you ain't workin', all you're doin' is stayin' indoors lookin' after me. You could use a night out."

"I—I was thinking about maybe going out later," she said in a funny sort of way.

"Good," Cash said, puzzled by her tone but not commenting on it.

Being so close to Lucinda over these past weeks, Cash had gotten to know her moods. Usually she was cheerful, or seemed to be. Today, though, he could sense that something was definitely troubling her. She hadn't come back in the same mood she'd left the house.

It was a quiet supper. Cash was hungry and wolfed down his meal, while Lucinda only picked at hers.

After supper Cash offered to help her clean up the dishes, which he usually did, if only to keep himself occupied. But she said she didn't want help and told him just to go sit and relax in the parlor. By now Cash was concerned enough to demand from her what was the matter. But he resisted and instead added more whiskey to his glass and went into the next room.

After the dishes were washed, Lucinda disappeared into the bedroom to change her clothes. Cash was frankly surprised to see that she really *was* planning to go out. It wasn't something that she would normally do. He'd made the suggestion to her before, and she always rejected it, preferring to stay in with him: talking, playing cards, or just cuddling together on the sofa. As Cash waited for her to come out, he smoked a couple of cigarettes and again debated whether he should talk to her. Something was not right— and, if it concerned her, chances were it probably involved him.

Lucinda came out. She was wearing a blue gingham dress and a heavy wool sweater. She'd even fussed with putting a ribbon in her hair. She seemed to be avoiding Cash as she went into the kitchen to find something to busy herself with.

At about seven o'clock she got ready to leave the house— again without saying a word to Cash.

He got up from the rocker and walked over to her while she stood at the door. She looked up at him quickly, furtively, but Cash noticed the briefest flicker of panic in her eyes. He took her firmly by the shoulders and demanded, "Lucinda, what's wrong?"

She started to speak but then began twisting her head, as if to physically stop herself from saying anything.

"Lucinda—"

"Please. I have to go."

"No," Cash said. "Not until you tell me—"

And at that moment the front door swung open.

Standing on the threshold with a broad grin stretched across his thin lips was Cash's one-time friend and now betrayer: The Whiskey Kid.

Steve Reno.

Chapter Twelve

I said we'd be here by seven," Steve said to Lucinda as he stepped inside the house. "And like my compadre here knows, I make it a point always to be on time."

To say Cash was startled wouldn't be telling it all. He pulled back from Lucinda. He looked at her squarely in the eyes but didn't know what his face was registering. Though it now became clear to him why Lucinda had acted so strangely tonight. She had arranged this. She'd set him up for Steve. Cash tried to speak, but no words would come.

Steve stood there, looking amused at Cash's dilemma. But any humor in the moment was lost on Cash—especially when the immense, imposing figure of Slug Fletcher materialized from around the outer doorway and fixed him with that familiar, black, dead-eyed stare.

"Don't hold it ag'in the girl, Cash," Steve said. "She really cares for you. In fact, she never hadda tell us where you were. We knew. Sure, remember a coupla nights before we robbed the stage? I wanted to keep an eye on you. So I had Andy Chelsea trail you. Yeah, Andy ain't much of a talker, but his redskin blood makes him a good tracker and an even better shadow. So when I heard that you might not be dead, I figgered there was a good chance you might come back here to lay low. Your gal only confirmed it. With a little persuasion."

Cash swiftly turned to Lucinda. "Did they—" he started to say.

"Take it easy, Cash," Steve said smoothly. "If I'd wanted to go rough on her, I'da let Slug handle the persuadin'. Let's just say I told her it was in your best interest that we get together."

"I—I'm sorry, Cash," Lucinda said, her voice quavering, eyes pleading for forgiveness.

Cash now knew it wasn't her fault. Steve in his typically conniving manner had forced her into a corner. But Cash still felt somehow betrayed.

Steve said, "Woulda come sooner, but I figgered there wasn't no rush. If you was here, you wouldn't be goin' anywhere for a while."

Cash turned and started back into the parlor for his drink. His mind was focused on a single thought: inside the bottom drawer of the bureau was where he'd placed his Colt .44, loaded with the four remaining bullets. If only he had the chance to get to it.

But Steve had followed him into the parlor, and Slug stood watching from the entrance hall.

Cash allowed himself his first good look at Steve. He looked sharp, as usual, well groomed, dressed in a tailored dark suit with red vest and wearing the cream-colored Stetson with the black band he'd taken to donning since coming out of Bennetsville. As Cash's eyes dipped, he also noticed a big, red-jeweled gold ring on his finger. A costly trinket that he sure hadn't picked up at the general store.

"Bein' a free man's agreed with you," Cash said with barely concealed contempt.

Steve eyed him flatly and ignored the comment.

"Okay, Steve," Cash said, maintaining his composure, "just say what you're here for."

Steve reached into his inside coat pocket and withdrew a gold cigarette case. He studied Cash under hooded eyes as he lit his cigarette by striking a match against the underside of the coffee table.

He blew out a cloud of smoke and spoke amicably. "You're in trouble, compadre. And I wanna help."

"You got no interest in helpin' me," Cash said through pursed lips.

Steve looked a little hurt at his lack of appreciation. "Siddown, Cash."

What choice did he have? He glanced over at poor Lucinda,

who looked stricken, and sat himself down on the sofa. Steve remained standing, lifting a boot onto the coffee table and looking down at Cash. A position he clearly relished.

Without turning his head he said to Slug, "Take the girl for a walk. I wanna talk to Cash alone."

Lucinda began to protest, but Cash gave her a reassuring look. He couldn't very well do anything else.

"And Slug . . . be nice to her," Steve added, smiling deviously for Cash's benefit.

Steve waited until they were gone from the house before he began talking. His words were not what Cash expected to hear.

"I did wrong by you, compadre. Now I wanna make it up to you."

Cash cast him an understandably dubious look.

"Yeah, I'm sure you do," he said, a little boldly.

Steve's expression remained set and serious. "I ain't foolin'. That job we pulled put me in good with my partners. They want to set me up in business in Laramie. Running one of their gamblin' halls. Legitimate all the way."

"I can't see you goin' honest, Steve," Cash remarked.

Steve rubbed a hurried finger under his sharp, arched nose. "Don't really matter what *you* see. But I'm offerin' you the chance to come in with me."

"For old times' sake?" Cash said sardonically.

"That how you see it?" Steve returned.

"Even if I trusted your offer, I'm a hunted man," Cash reminded him.

Steve brushed that concern aside. "You ain't so well known in Laramie. And by the time we get this thing up and operatin', Cash McCall will be dead and forgotten. And if'n there should be any trouble . . . don't forget, I got partners who can fix just 'bout anything."

Cash had to confess, he was intrigued, in a skeptical sort of way.

But he still had to have his say.

"First you set me up—and real good, by the way . . . now you wanna work me into this deal of yours. Don't add up, Steve."

"Reckon lookin' at it from your side, it don't," Steve agreed. "But lemme just say there's a reason for what happened."

Cash smirked disdainfully. "That I'd like to hear."

Steve didn't acknowledge the comment. Instead he said, "You kept your mouth shut. You coulda told the sheriff your story when he almost brung you in. After all, you got nothin' to lose. A noose'll fit 'round my neck as easily as it will yours."

"How do you know I didn't talk to the sheriff?" Cash said craftily.

"I'm still walkin' the streets," Steve answered simply.

"You got nothin' to lose, either, Steve," Cash said.

Steve took a final puff from his cigarette before butting it in the ashtray.

"True," he said contemplatively. "But then, you *might* get to talkin', and I can't afford no suspicion fallin' on me now."

Steve was using all the persuasive tricks Cash knew him for. But it wasn't hard for him to see through Reno's "sincerity." Steve didn't owe him a damn thing, and he knew it. Cash didn't trust him or his offer. He figured Steve had to have something else in mind. Cash was the one guy who could bring him trouble with what he knew about the Wells Fargo holdup. And while it would have been simpler for Steve just to kill him, he seemed to have come up with another plan to keep Cash in line.

Cash sat quietly, smoking a fresh cigarette, while he considered his options. What it boiled down to was that he had none. He had to at least pretend to go along with what Steve was offering. There were two reasons that decided him. First, if he refused, he was surely a dead man. Second, he had Lucinda to consider. Lucinda, who at that moment was walking the streets with the most deadly thug in Wyoming.

"Feel like gettin' out tonight?" Steve asked next.

"Hardly," Cash replied with an ironic edge.

Steve spoke with assurance. "You don't gotta worry. Sheriff and his posse are still out trackin' you. They went out yesterday and, from what I heard, won't be back for a coupla days. He wants to get this cleared up 'fore the snows come. He's dead set on findin' you, Cash. You're his prize. Yeah, so I figgered we could head down to Molly's and maybe have a coupla drinks and talk a little more. You can't wanna be cooped up in here any longer. And Molly's is one place you know you'll be safe."

"Yeah?" Cash said, not hiding his suspicion.

Steve said smoothly: "If I'd wanted another shot at you, compadre, I coulda sent Slug or Andy in here anytime. But it's a different game now. Question is, are you willin' to play?"

"Reckon I ain't got much say," Cash said with a sigh.

Steve looked pleased. "Got my carriage out front. It's dark—no one will see you. We'll ride the rear road and go in through the back way."

"What 'bout Lu—the girl?" Cash wanted to know.

"She stays here. Our business is strictly 'tween us."

They waited until Slug came back from his walk with Lucinda. She looked scared, and her body was trembling a little when Cash saw her enter the house, the result of an evening stroll with Slug Fletcher. He didn't lessen her apprehension when he told her he would be going out with Steve. Naturally she didn't want him to, though she realized he had no choice. Cash told her with as much confidence as he could muster that he wouldn't be long, and Steve confirmed it.

As if Lucinda would trust Steve Reno any more than Cash would . . .

The carriage was parked in back of the house. The autumn night had fallen like a black curtain, and in the darkness, seated in the backseat under the fringed canopy, Cash would be well concealed from any citizen onlooker they might pass. Steve sat next to him while Slug took over the reins. Cash did appreciate getting out into the cool, crisp autumn air—though he definitely would have preferred different company.

They rode toward the saloon in silence. Cash took that time to reflect on all that had happened since his release from Bennetsville. His kid brother had been sentenced to his own term in prison for robbery and assault. Ma had taken sick and died. He had participated in a robbery that left five people dead and that saw himself set up as the scapegoat by someone he'd considered a friend. And now tonight he was heading out with that "friend" to shoot back a few drinks and discuss a business deal.

Yeah, his *friend,* to whom Cash owed a blood debt he would soon pay in full.

To complete the picture, Cash had met and was starting to feel a strong affection for Lucinda, the one bright spot in a mess of bad breaks.

At least he hoped she was.

While his mother had been a churchgoing woman, Cash himself never gave much thought to God or grace or mercy. He'd always been a believer in fate. As they rode that night, he couldn't help thinking that the Fates must have been having a good laugh at his expense.

They arrived at Dead Eye Molly's and climbed out of the carriage at the rear door of the saloon. It wasn't a customer entrance; it was the private door that Molly used to enter and exit her living quarters, where she wouldn't put herself on display for the good folks who might pass by on the street and continue to shun her because of her deformed eye.

The door was unlocked, and the three went into the saloon through the corridor. Molly wasn't around, and when Cash asked, Steve said she was passed out drunk in her room, which was her nightly ritual. Cash had a feeling Steve had contributed to that, possibly for his own benefit. Steve was always taking precautions. Maybe he wasn't sure he could trust Molly once she saw Cash. The reward offered for his capture was a mighty big temptation, especially to a money-grubber like Molly Ferguson.

The saloon looked empty, as it had been that night Cash had gone there to meet with Steve to ask for his help. But as they went to the dark corner table where Steve preferred to sit, Cash wasn't happy to see Andy Chelsea already seated there, regarding him with that kill-you-if-I-could look that had become all too familiar to Cash.

There was a fresh bottle of whiskey on the table. Once they took their chairs, Steve poured each of them a drink. Cash felt tight and uncomfortable, his tenseness not relieved when Steve lifted his glass to toast their "partnership."

Cash didn't rush to raise his glass. Instead he risked either a bullet from Slug or a knife in the back from Andy Chelsea when he asked Steve outright: "Why'd you double-cross me, Steve?"

Steve's answer was to the point, as if he'd been expecting the question, but his voice held no trace of guilt or remorse.

"It was business, compadre. Just business."

"Business," Cash snorted. "Where you set me up and left me for dead."

Steve kept his eyes steady on Cash. "Friendships don't mean nothin' in that kind of a deal. Sure, I regretted what I done, and whether or not you wanna believe me, I'm glad you're alive and sittin' here, sharin' a drink. But I was given the orders from my partners. Someone had to be left behind."

"And McGraw?"

Steve leaned forward and held his whiskey glass in both hands, gazing thoughtfully into the amber alcohol. "Part of the arrangement."

Cash shifted in his chair. "So there was never them skinners to take the blame?"

Steve sat back and rubbed a hand under his chin. "Couldn't rightly tell you that, could I?"

Cash couldn't explain why, but he had the sudden uneasy feeling that at any moment he was a dead man. Maybe it was because Steve was coming clean with him. Or perhaps the setting was too perfect. Three murderers seated around him and not a single witness in the place.

Before he could contemplate that disturbing possibility any further, Steve spoke up.

"So what d'you wanna do 'bout it, Cash? Do you think you can fight me? Or my partners? You can't be that dumb to think you can win."

Cash could see that Steve was becoming heated and wrestling to keep his temper in check. He didn't want their "friendly" talk to turn ugly.

Even though Cash might have been playing a dangerous hand, he felt he had the right to have his say. He was owed that, at least.

But again realizing how easy it would be for Steve or one of his pair of killers to "silence" him, he decided not to provoke them.

"All right, Steve," he said. "I ain't lookin' for a fight."

Cash didn't know if Steve believed him. He certainly wasn't trying to convince himself. Hell, he was lying through his teeth.

Steve spoke pensively. "We go back a long way, compadre. Done a lot together. A coupla real hell-raisers in our time. Yet we always stuck by each other. Tight—like this." He locked the fingers of his hands together for emphasis. "Then I go and put a bullet into you and leave you behind to take the heat. You got every reason to wanna see me dead."

"I said to forget it," Cash said with emphasis.

"Yeah, well, that's the thing," Steve said, darkly reflective, rocking his head slowly. "You seem too willing to forget. If'n it was you that done that to me, I'd be out to cut your throat."

Cash felt his insides start to crawl. Why was Steve telling him this? Was it a threat, the warning rattle of a snake before it strikes? All he kept thinking was that it would be simple for Steve to finish what he'd started at Taylor's Pass.

Perhaps Steve noticed his discomfort, because his mood lightened.

"Take it easy, Cash," he said. "I just gotta know where we stand with each other. You're the one person who stands 'tween me and a noose. Okay, maybe I missed my chance. Call me superstitious, but I gotta leave it at that."

Steve Reno, superstitious? In a pig's eye.

Cash took another chance with his words. But he knew that Steve wouldn't trust him unless he was completely honest with him—or at least as honest as Cash was prepared to be.

"Steve, after what you done, cuttin' your throat would be too good for you. You want the truth, that's it. I ain't never gonna trust you. But I reckon that goes both ways."

Steve looked impressed, and after several seconds his mouth broadened in a grin. He lifted his glass. "That's what I wanted to hear you say, compadre. Y'know, I heard it said once that bitterness will kill you faster than a bullet. Not trustin' each other . . . that's a different matter."

Cash's stomach settled, but his body was tense with a barely restrained rage. Steve couldn't guess at the hatred that festered inside of him. The longer Cash sat with him, the more desperately he wanted to remove Reno's stain from the fabric of his life.

Steve added more whiskey to Cash's glass. He again raised his own in a toast. This time Cash slowly lifted his—and resisted every urge just to toss the liquor into Steve's lying, treacherous face.

Steve then reached into his shirt pocket and carelessly withdrew a handful of bills that he slapped down on the table and pushed across to Cash.

"Makes up for nothin'," he said. "Consider it a show of goodwill."

Cash regarded the money with an empty expression. Maybe a couple hundred dollars. Nowhere near what Steve owed him. But he took the money without a word and jammed it into his pants pocket.

Steve seemed satisfied. Then his face took on a peculiar look, as if he'd just reminded himself of something.

"There's just one thing more, Cash," he said matter-of-factly. "A final detail to seal our arrangement."

Cash didn't like the sound of that. That was another moment when he felt his nerves tense, half expecting another double-cross. Maybe a quick bullet to the head, courtesy of Slug.

Instead Steve got up from his chair and ambled over to stand at the opening to the corridor, where he looked to be gesturing to someone. Soon a figure stepped out from the corridor, appearing as little more than a shadow. The two then walked directly to where Cash was sitting. As soon as they moved into the dim light that splashed over the table, Cash felt as if he'd been blasted by a double load of buckshot.

Steve's grin resembled that of a shark within reach of its prey as he said, "I want you should meet one of our new boys."

Standing next to Steve Reno was Ethan McCall.

Chapter Thirteen

In his astonishment Cash could hardly recognize his kid brother. He was dressed in the style associated with Steve. A sharp, tailored suit and vest, clean white shirt complemented by a bolo tie. He was even sporting a derby, tipped at a rakish angle. Without any question Cash was looking at Steve Reno's protégé. Fashioned in his own image.

When Ethan's eyes connected with his brother, it was with scarce familiarity. He looked right through Cash as if he were a stranger, all the time with a cigarette hanging limply from the corner of his mouth.

"Glad to see me, brother?" he said tonelessly, working his words around his smoke.

Cash's eyes veered toward Steve. Steve Reno couldn't have looked any more pleased at their "reunion."

"My partners got him out 'bout a month ago, compadre," he explained. "Reckon I wasn't exactly tellin' the truth when I said nothing could be done for him. Fact is, good behavior and a little of the right influence, and the prison was more than happy to let a good kid like Ethan out. 'Course we couldn't leave him to fend for himself, so we sorta brought him in with us."

The blood surged into Cash's throat, and he could barely mutter, "You low-down skunk."

"Careful, compadre," Steve warned smoothly.

Cash knew he had to keep a rein on his temper and tried to calm himself.

"You rather the kid rot in prison for another year?" Steve said, speaking as if he had done Cash a favor.

"He'll rot all right," Cash said thickly.

"Take it easy, Cash," Ethan said. "I owe Steve."

Cash knew he'd get nowhere with the kid by normal reasoning, so he attempted another approach.

"Kid, what would Ma say?" he said plaintively.

"The old lady's dead," Ethan said coldly.

Ethan's callous remark triggered a harsh response from his brother.

"Yeah, she's dead. And you helped kill her."

Ethan's body stiffened like a rod, and his pretty face reddened as the hot flow of blood rushed into his head. He made a lunge at his brother. Instinctively, Cash leaped to his feet to meet him. He didn't even wait for Ethan to take the first swing. He threw a hard punch to his gut that doubled the kid over. Then, with his blood racing at a fury, Cash grabbed him by his coat lapels, tugged him upright, and punched him directly in the face. Everyone heard his nose crack as a fountain of blood erupted from Ethan's nostrils, pouring out onto his fancy new suit. Ethan staggered back and dropped to his knees, cupping both hands under his nose to catch the flow.

"Thecond time you hit me like that, Cath," he said, sputtering and slurring his words. "Now you went and broke my nothe, you dirty fink. Thith time I won't be forgettin'."

His anger spent, Cash shifted his gaze from Ethan to Steve— and waited to see what his nemesis would do. Steve's response wasn't terribly surprising. His mouth widened in a grin.

"Dissension in the ranks," he applauded.

Cash gave him a dirty look as he swept the back of his hand across his sweaty brow.

Steve spoke with a bit more seriousness. "Slug, get the kid cleaned up. He might need a doctor, but don't tell nothin' that happened. That goes for you too, kid. Keep your mouth shut. Just a nice neighborly brawl. Nothin' more. And, Ethan, one more thing: don't be callin' your brother a fink. A fink is a belly-crawler who rats out his friends." He cast his eyes toward Cash and said in a deliberate tone, "And Cash is too smart for that."

After Slug and Ethan disappeared into the back where the

washing area was, Steve walked up close to Cash, his head lowered, busily scratching behind his ear.

"You likely ruined the kid's face," he said without concern.

"Somethin' I shoulda done a long time ago," Cash said.

"It'll give the kid some character," Steve remarked. "Always figgered Ethan was too purty."

"You pulled a real smart move, Steve," Cash said tightly.

Steve twisted the meaning of Cash's words around. "Yeah. I feel the kid's got some possibilities."

"You know what I mean. Now you got yourself an insurance policy," Cash added.

"One way of lookin' at it," Steve agreed with a slight nod. "But let's say now that you know how things are, I feel a mite more comfortable 'bout our arrangement."

Cash challenged him. "And what if I told you I don't give a damn what happens to the kid?"

"That the way you feel, Cash?" Steve said slowly, a knowing glint in his eye.

Cash didn't have to say anything. Steve knew the truth.

Steve yawned and stretched his arms back over his shoulders. "Well, enough fun for one night. Time for you to be gettin' back to your girl. I'll ride you in the carriage."

Cash shook his head. "I'll walk."

Steve shrugged but spoke with mock concern. "Not smart, compadre. You got a mighty handsome reward on your head."

"Why don't you collect it, Steve?" Cash said with wry contempt.

Cash walked away and left the saloon through the back way, slinking back to Lucinda and a semblance of sanity under the protective cover of darkness.

Cash did have to hand it to him: Steve had pulled a clever stunt. He'd gotten to Ethan where the kid was the most vulnerable, showing him the big money and fancy living. And what could Cash do about it? He was on the dodge, a guy with either a bullet or a rope in his future. No, The Whiskey Kid was the one for the kid to look up to now.

There was only one way to set things straight, Cash told himself as he edged through the night shadows to the big house. What he'd already determined he must do. He had to kill Steve Reno—and now not only to satisfy his need for vengeance, but to protect his kid brother.

When Cash got back to the house, he found Lucinda waiting up for him. She looked relieved that he had gotten home safely, but it was clear she was still dealing with her own guilt. She immediately felt she had to explain what had happened earlier. Even though it wasn't necessary—Cash knew all that he had to—Lucinda was insistent.

He felt sorry for her and so sat beside her on the sofa. She took his hands and told him how when she had gone out shopping for groceries that afternoon, she'd been accosted by Slug Fletcher, who took her into an alley where Steve Reno was waiting. Steve had spoken to the point, saying that if she didn't come clean about Cash hiding out at the house, he and Slug would pay their own visit one night. Lucinda said the look on the big man's face was so frightening, she knew the threat was real.

After she was done, Lucinda squeezed Cash's hands tightly and said, "I would never betray you, Cash. But they didn't leave me a choice."

Cash believed her story—and he believed her. He told her that there was nothing else she could have done. If she hadn't confessed to his being there, Steve surely would have made good on his threat. Cash had seen firsthand what Steve Reno and his gang were capable of.

Now more relaxed with Cash's reassurance that he understood, Lucinda tentatively asked him about his meeting with Steve. Cash didn't want to say more than he had to and chance worrying her any more than he already had. Because of his choosing her house to recuperate and hide out in after he'd been shot, Lucinda had learned more than Cash ever wanted her to. What Cash feared most was that, unless he went along completely with Steve, Lucinda, too, might find herself in a threatened situation.

But he also realized that because Lucinda *was* now involved, it wouldn't be fair or right to hold anything back from her. What he would tell her would not be pleasant, but she should know what they were up against.

They sat at the kitchen table, where they both had some whiskey to relax themselves. Cash started off by telling Lucinda about the neat trick Steve had pulled with his brother, adding, "Steve's put himself at an advantage. But he's gotta know I aim to kill him."

Lucinda was understanding, though noticeably apprehensive.

She lowered her lashes and spoke into her glass. "I don't want to think about you killing anyone." Then she looked up, straight into Cash's eyes. "But more than that, I don't want to see you dead."

"Honey, it's gotta be one way or the other," Cash replied with an open gesturing of his hands.

Lucinda wore a pained expression. "I saw those men, and I can't forget what you told me . . . about what they did to those people on the stagecoach. That poor girl," she said, her fingers reflexively tightening around her glass. "I know what they're capable of. If they feel threatened by you—"

Cash interrupted her. "But they won't do nothin'," he said reassuringly. "Not right away, 'leastwise. That's why Steve brought my brother into this. As long as he's got Ethan, he knows he can call the shots." As he considered that, his temper flared, and he suddenly pounded a fist onto the table, hard enough to rattle the two drinking glasses.

"Dumb kid!" he said spitefully. "He saw how it was for me. Didn't mean a thing to him. All he can see are fancy clothes and dollar signs. Yeah, Steve's corralled him real good."

Lucinda knew he needed to let off that steam and didn't react. But when he looked over at her, his expression was a trifle embarrassed. He smiled self-consciously.

A few moments later Lucinda suddenly yawned. She swiftly pressed a hand over her mouth, embarrassed to have Cash see that she was tired after all that he had gone through that day.

He smiled understandingly. "It's been a helluva day," he said. "Why don't you get some shut-eye?"

"I'm all right," she protested.

Cash stood and helped her up from her chair. "No, you're tuckered out. And I ain't in the mood for no arguments."

Lucinda looked at Cash with a soft affection in her eyes. "I want you to be careful, Cash. But whatever you decide to do, I'm beside you."

Cash kissed her tenderly on the cheek. "Go on," he said.

When she was gone, Cash casually reached a hand into his pants pocket and felt a crumple of paper. He'd forgotten all about the "handout" Steve had given him. He pulled out the bills and looked hard at the money. Money that had once seemed so important to Cash now looked dirty and meaningless. He didn't even want to be holding it, knowing how each bill was marked with blood and stained by betrayal. Disgusted, he threw the cash onto the table.

He knew that he wouldn't get any sleep, so he walked into the parlor. He parted the curtains just a bit and peered out into the night. The autumn moon was full and low, and he watched as a rolling cloud bank lazily passed before it, drifting off into the west.

The night was peaceful.

But Cash wondered what the new day would bring.

Chapter Fourteen

The following day passed uneventfully. As evening approached and it came time for Lucinda to get ready for her shift at the coffee shop, she confessed to Cash that she was afraid to leave him alone and offered to stay home from work. Cash quickly dismissed the idea. He told her it wouldn't be smart for her to interrupt her routine, and that he would be fine. There was nothing she could do in any case. And, while Cash didn't voice it, if there should be any trouble tonight, he wanted her away. But Cash wasn't too worried about her safety; he hadn't given Steve reason to start threatening her. Besides, Steve already had his ace in the hole with his brother.

Still, Cash wasn't taking any chances. He waited until Lucinda had gone. Then, for the first time since he'd gotten there, he strapped on the gun belt he'd kept in the bottom drawer of the bureau. He wasn't ready to make his move against Steve just yet, but he had every intention of protecting himself should Steve decide to make the first move.

Come around nine o'clock, Cash heard pronounced footfalls on the porch followed by a heavy knock on the door. He wasn't surprised; was, in fact, expecting the visit. What did surprise him was that it wasn't Steve Reno who appeared on the doorstep but Slug Fletcher. Alone.

Cash let Slug do the talking.

"Steve wants to see ya. At Molly's."

Cash merely gave his head a nod. As with the night before, what choice did he have but to go along? He went to get his Stetson, then followed Slug out back to the buggy.

He felt like a night crawler, sneaking out after dark and riding in back of the buggy while Slug drove the unoccupied back routes to the saloon. Lucinda would be home shortly after ten, weekday closing time at the coffee shop, and Cash was concerned that when she didn't find him there, she'd worry. But he trusted that after their talk last night, she understood he would have to bide his time and play the game by Steve's rules.

Until the moment was right.

When they entered the saloon through their usual back entrance, Cash was startled to see Molly standing inside the hall outside the open door to her room, puffing on a pipe. She wasn't supposed to know about his being in town. She glared at Cash out of her good eye but didn't say a word. She led the two men into the saloon.

The front door was locked, and there were no other customers. Just Steve sitting at his usual table, surrounded by his boys, who now included Ethan, who was seated at Steve's right. The kid looked at Cash coldly, his eyes shooting daggers. He had a bandage covering his broken nose.

Steve's attention instantly fell upon Cash's gun belt and holstered Colt revolver.

"See you're heeled," he said with a thin smile. "'Spectin' trouble, compadre?"

Cash didn't answer.

Slug stood behind him, waiting for Cash to take his chair. Cash didn't care to sit next to his brother, whose tight stare was a clear invitation for Cash to keep his distance, so he reluctantly took the chair beside Andy Chelsea, who was slouched in his seat, picking at his fingernails with a large knife. Andy just raised his cruel eyes to Cash for an instant before he went back to his idling.

Cash half turned toward the bar. Molly was just standing there, watching them with a miserable look on her ugly face. Once everyone was seated, the room became as quiet as a funeral parlor.

Finally Steve broke the silence. He leaned forward in his chair and glanced first at Ethan, then at Cash.

"Look at the two of you," he said. "You're blood, and you both look like you wanna kill each other."

Cash could scarcely believe what he was hearing. Steve was

the one who had brought him and his brother to this point, and now he was trying to make peace between them?

But it soon became clear to him. Of course Steve didn't want them to be at odds. He wouldn't have the leverage he wanted unless he could be certain Cash cared about what happened to the kid. And maybe he still had a bit of doubt that Cash didn't give a damn.

"How 'bout you boys shakin' hands, huh?" Steve said.

Ethan's eyes shifted toward Cash, but there was no warmth in them. Cash couldn't afford to be angry with his brother if he was hoping to lure him away from Steve and his influence . . . so he willingly extended his hand across the table. Ethan coldly ignored his gesture.

"He's offerin' you his hand, kid," Steve said sternly.

Ethan hesitated for several moments, then relented and met Cash's hand in a quick, weak grip.

Not the warmest or most sincere handshake in the world. But it seemed to satisfy Steve.

"That's better," he said. "Now we can open a bottle and do us a little celebratin'."

Steve reached for the whiskey bottle and began pouring each of his men a drink. Ethan put a hand over his glass, complaining, "I can't taste nothin'."

"Yeah, a busted nose'll do that to you," Steve said idly, sucking a tooth.

"Is that the only reason you sent for me?" Cash asked Steve directly.

Steve's look was uncomprehending, though Cash was certain he knew what he meant.

"To get me and Ethan to make up," he clarified.

"Can't a few pals get together for a coupla drinks?" Steve returned innocently.

"So that's the way it's gonna be," Cash said with a slow, knowing nod. The meaning behind Steve's comment was not so subtle that Cash couldn't read into it. He wanted his band close to him—particularly Cash.

Steve pierced Cash with his deep-set eyes, and his tone hardened. "Yeah, Cash. Before we make our move to Laramie, I might get a yen to have us pals together for a drink at our old watering hole. You ain't got a problem with that, have you?"

He wasn't asking Cash; he was *telling* him the way it was going to be. To make certain Cash understood, he made sure that Cash was facing him as he quickly shifted his eyes toward Ethan.

Steve could not have made his point any more clear.

And through it all Ethan sat there accepting that he was a part of Steve's gang. Completely ignorant of the *real* part he was playing. A mere toy to be manipulated by Steve Reno at his whim. And what could Cash say that would convince his brother otherwise? He was certain that Steve in his cleverness had turned the kid so against him that anything Cash said wouldn't amount to snake spit.

They drank for most of the night, and though Cash tried to be careful to keep on his guard, the steady flow of liquor was hitting him pretty hard. His lack of sleep only intensified the effects. He figured that was Steve's plan, to get the gang loosened up sufficiently so everyone would stay friendly. He even livened up his party by inviting some saloon girls to drop by, but Cash kept a distance. When it came to that kind of companionship, he kept thinking of Lucinda, soon to be waiting with uncertainty at the house.

Steve, of course, took full advantage of the girls' company, as did Ethan. It troubled Cash to watch his brother try to follow Steve's example with these much older and "experienced" women, especially when he thought back to the sweet young gal who had become so distraught the night Ethan and his pals were arrested outside the pool room. At the same time, Cash was glad she was out of Ethan's life now. He wouldn't want a girl like that to be with what his brother had become.

By midnight everyone was in pretty bad shape, except for Slug, who had an enormous capacity for liquor. Andy looked to be passed out facedown on the table, but he'd periodically revive long enough to let out a war whoop that rang throughout the saloon. Cash just wanted to get the hell out of there, but Steve made it clear he wasn't ready to break up his little party. And he further made it understood that Cash was his "guest."

Cash's bladder soon called with an urgency that he had to

acknowledge. He lifted himself from his chair and started out back to relieve himself. Molly was at the bar, and when she saw Cash heading in that direction, she followed him into the corridor. Cash could tell she had something to say. Something he assumed by her determined posture that she'd been waiting for just this opportunity to tell him.

She'd become more hunched over since Cash had last seen her, and with her patch-covered eye and overall ugly appearance, she reminded him of a freak in a traveling show. Her ornery mood completed the effect.

She stopped Cash before he reached the back door and asked for a cigarette. Cash gave her his pouch and papers to build her own. Molly waited until her smoke was lit and she could take a few deep inhales before she began talking. Although Cash's bladder was close to bursting, he was patient.

"I know what The Kid done to ya," she said in her hoarse, throaty voice. "And I want ya to know he wasn't fair to old Molly, neither."

Cash could smell the heavy odor of rotgut and tobacco roll off her breath, made worse by the stench of her rotten teeth. He tried to step back from her, but she took him by his sore arm and held firm.

"He's got a mittful of money, The Kid does," she went on. "But does he cut Molly in on his deal? No, he don't. He forgets how I used to help you boys when no one else would. He forgets 'bout his friends . . . like you found out, eh?"

Although Cash was feeling his liquor, he still had enough of his wits about him to know it wasn't smart for Molly to be talking like that. Regardless of his own feelings toward Steve, Cash couldn't sympathize with Molly's complaint. Steve didn't owe her anything. She'd never done anything special for him. She treated Steve no differently from any of her other customers when she'd handle his stolen goods—paying him pennies on the dollar the way she did with every other small-time thief.

Cash warned Molly to keep her mouth shut. As greedy as that old crone was, Steve was a whole lot greedier—and meaner. He wouldn't let anything come between him and a buck and would just as soon close that gap with a bullet.

But Molly's drunkenness made her defiant. "You think I won't be tellin' that punk—The Whiskey Kid, he calls himself—what I think of him? He plays the big shot 'round here, havin' me shut down my business so him and his—his *friends* can drink my whiskey." Her voice became maudlin. "But you, McCall . . . you ain't like him and his scum. And you know I run a respectable business. Not a gatherin' place for hoodlums."

Molly started to sway, and Cash swiftly grabbed her by the shoulders to steady her. He could sense trouble brewing, and the only way he might prevent it was by getting Molly into her room to sleep it off.

Cash tried to be gentle, but she started to wrestle against him, repeating in a loud voice how he had to let her go so she could settle things with Steve once and for all. For a quick moment Cash even considered laying one on her chin to quiet her and put her out for the night. She finally broke free of his grip and staggered into the saloon.

Cash watched her go. He couldn't stop her. Even if he could have halted her tonight, she'd be sure to get drunk on another occasion and make her point with Steve. Cash just shook his head and stepped outside to empty his bladder.

The night was crisp, and it felt good to be outdoors after breathing in the smoky, stale air that hung heavily in the saloon. Cash was in no rush to go back inside and decided just to sit and enjoy the cool and the quiet for a while. Clear his head a bit before getting himself the hell away from there. He moved to the back of the building where it was particularly dark and sat against the wall.

He got himself settled and almost instantly passed out for a time, which, when he came to, he realized hadn't been a smart thing. Even though Garrett O'Dowd wouldn't be returning until sometime tomorrow, Cash still risked being spotted by a late passerby. Then he relaxed. Drunks lying unconscious outside of Dead Eye Molly's were a common sight, and no one cared to bother with them. If anyone had seen him, they'd probably just think he was another casualty of Molly's bad whiskey.

When his eyes had blearily opened, he had one hell of a headache, and his stomach was churning from all the liquor he had ingested. He just wanted to go home and to bed but thought he'd better check on his brother first. Most of what he remembered was a blur. The last thing he recalled was Molly going off to confront Steve. Cash could well imagine how that little talk had gone.

When he entered the saloon through the back corridor, it appeared to be empty. The saloon girls had gone. The only light came from a corner kerosene lamp affixed to the wall beside the table where the group had been sitting. Cash saw Steve—sitting there alone. He stumbled over to him.

"Thought you'd gone," Steve said morosely.

It was strange. From what Cash could remember, Steve had drunk as much as any of them. But now he was seated upright in his chair, groomed and looking as sober as a judge. The only difference was that he didn't look as amiable as he had earlier. The expression on his face was set and grim. And he was watching Cash. Not with any kind of intent, just as if he were simply his point of focus. It was an eerie tableau.

Cash stood across from him, bracing himself steady by clasping his hands around the edge of the table.

"Where's my brother?" he demanded in a whiskey-slurred voice.

Steve never liked to talk to anyone who was standing taller than he was.

"Siddown, 'fore you fall over," he said.

"I asked you, where's Ethan?" Cash repeated, more emphatically.

"He left with the boys. Went back to the hotel."

"What . . . Y'got him livin' with you?" Cash said belligerently.

"Shut up, compadre," Steve said in a perfectly calm voice.

In his alcohol-fueled state Cash became bold. "Y-you just remember, Steve. You can't be talkin' to me like no big shot. I know things too."

"Yeah?" Steve smiled. He was as amused by Cash's drunken bravado as he seemed unconcerned by it.

Cash decided he'd be wise to shut up. With the liquor still loosening his tongue, it was too easy to start saying the wrong things.

"Where's Molly?" he asked in a less aggressive voice.

"Yeah, Molly," Steve said with a thoughtful nod. "Told me you and her was talkin' a bit."

"Told her she's gotta watch that she don't talk too much," Cash blurted.

"You did?"

Cash rocked his head loosely.

Steve smiled a slow smile. "She musta appreciated you tellin' her that, compadre. 'Cause she left somethin' for you."

Cash squinted, trying to focus his blurred vision. "Yeah? What?"

Steve held his smile and steadied his eyes on Cash as he reached into his shirt pocket and withdrew something that he kept hidden in a closed fist. Then he twisted his hand palm upright and slowly opened his fingers.

Cash looked into his hand . . . and sobered up faster than he had a right to.

Steve was holding Molly's eye patch.

Chapter Fifteen

Cash's face paled, and he felt his tender stomach start to heave. His legs were weak, and he collapsed heavily into the chair across from Steve.

His brain could hardly grasp the terrible truth, but the evidence was right before him.

It now made sense to Cash why Steve hadn't been concerned about Molly's seeing him that night. She would never say anything, even if she had a mind to. She'd be killed before the night was over.

Steve was completely composed. He put no more importance on that eye patch than if he were holding a grape. All he said was, "The old witch got greedy. Wanted a piece of the pie. Said if she didn't get it . . . well, you figger it out."

"She was *drunk!*" Cash exclaimed.

"Yeah," Steve sneered. "And she's always drunk. Drunk and bigmouthed. I don't know how she knew 'bout the job we pulled, but she did. Molly talked too much, and she saw too much. Now she won't be seein' nothin'."

Cash didn't know how Molly was killed or who had done it, and he didn't want to know. It was enough that he saw the evidence of one of the gang's handiwork.

"Anyway, that's one less concern I got." Steve looked Cash over. "You look terrible, compadre. You better get home and sleep it off."

But Cash didn't get home. With the liquor and this nightmare swirling around in his head, he blacked out in his chair.

It was daylight when he awoke. Faint rays of sunlight filtered into the saloon through the dark panes of glass. He still hadn't

146

completely sobered up and was mighty queasy in his belly. But that wasn't his main concern. He had to find some way of getting back to Lucinda without being noticed by anyone. Even the back alleys weren't safe for him in the daytime.

He was alone in the saloon. Steve had left him passed out in his chair—probably thinking it would be funny for him to wake there and discover his dilemma.

What wasn't so funny was Molly's bartender coming in to work, finding her missing, and seeing Cash sitting in the saloon alone. Cash didn't think the man knew about his two visits to the saloon with Steve, since he'd never been around at their gatherings. Steve and his boys served their own liquor when it was their party. But if the barkeep walked in now while Cash was still inside, Cash'd likely be in for a mess of trouble.

Once again, courtesy of Steve, Cash found himself caught in a sticky situation.

He checked the time on his pocket watch. Eight thirty-three. Still early. Might not be too many people out and about. With a little luck and a lot of caution, Cash figured he might be able to get himself back to Lucinda safely.

He left through the back door and scouted each direction carefully. He wore his Stetson low as he started down the back ways. He kept his gait as steady as his hungover condition allowed, so as not to arouse suspicion if someone should step out the back door of any of the business establishments along his route. It wasn't a long walk, only about fifteen minutes, but it seemed like an hour before Cash finally got to the house. He waited out back until some citizens passed by before he hurried up the porch to the door, hoping it was unlocked. Luckily it was.

Lucinda was waiting for him in the parlor, and from the tired and troubled look on her face it appeared that she hadn't gotten any sleep. But when she saw Cash, relief flooded her features, and she leaped up from the rocker and rushed over to embrace him. They held each other close for several minutes. Cash was never so glad to be with anyone. The way her arms were squeezing him, with more strength than he thought could come from a woman, he reckoned she felt the same way.

When Lucinda finally spoke, her voice still held trepidation.

"I thought something happened to you," she said. "That maybe . . ." She couldn't finish.

"Had a late-night caller," Cash explained as calmly as he was able. He didn't want any false note in his tone to alarm her. "Didn't have no choice 'cept to go along."

"Reno?" she asked.

He nodded. "Was him who sent for me."

They unlocked from their embrace and went to sit on the sofa. Cash was exhausted, both physically and emotionally, and wasn't ready to talk about what had happened at the saloon. But he had come to one conclusion, regarding Lucinda, and he gave it to her straight.

"Lucinda, I don't want you to stay here. Reno knows we're together, and if he plans a move ag'in me, I don't want you gettin' caught in the crossfire."

Lucinda's expression went rigid. "I'm not leaving you, Cash," she said adamantly.

"Listen," Cash said, shifting his body closer to her. "I gotta finish this 'fore Steve makes his move to Laramie, which could be any day now. Once he's there, I won't have no chance ag'in him, not with his partners backin' him. He's expectin' me to go with him, and if it comes to him bringin' Ethan along . . . I won't have no choice."

Lucinda's words came tentatively. "Is your brother . . . so important to you?"

Cash went silent. He didn't take offense at what she was saying. But that was rightly a question with no easy answer. And it got him to considering. If Steve got to him first, would Ethan even care? After what Cash had seen of Ethan, what he'd become under Steve Reno's influence, he doubted it. So why was he feeling such a responsibility for the kid?

Cash chewed on his lip and finally decided it best just not to answer her. Thankfully she didn't press the matter.

"I can't be leaving you alone to face this, Cash. I *won't*. How can I be off somewhere not knowing what might be happening to you?"

"It ain't what I want, neither," Cash assured her. "But I gotta know that Steve can't be gettin' to you."

Lucinda's mouth tightened. "At least tell me what you're going to do."

"Try to straighten this out with Ethan. Don't know how, but I gotta make him see that he's of no worth to Steve 'cept as a way to keep me close to him. Once I ain't a worry to Steve, Ethan won't have a dog's chance in hell. I know that. Steve needs his road clear to move on to what he's got with his partners in Laramie."

Lucinda asked her next question carefully. "Then . . . why hasn't he killed you already? Or, if he knew you were here, why didn't he simply go to the sheriff and turn you in?"

Cash huffed a quick exhale. "He wouldn't get the law involved. That'd be too easy and a mite risky for himself. He wants to settle this his own way. It's like some game he's playin'. Best I can figger is, he's waitin' for me to make the first move. That's why he's doin' all he can to provoke me. But not pushin' too hard. Not yet."

Lucinda sat upright on the sofa. "I still think you should go to the sheriff. Tell him what you know."

Cash considered only for an instant before he gave his head a definite shake.

He said, "O'Dowd would throw me into a cell faster than he'd toss a horseshoe. And even if he did believe me, he's got no proof, no evidence ag'in Steve. Just what I'd have to say, and my word ain't worth much. And once I was locked up . . . that'd be it for Ethan. He'd either disappear or have some convenient 'accident.' Then Steve wins all the way." He took a breath and stared hard and steadily at Lucinda. "I gotta do this alone. And you gotta see that."

Lucinda's face looked sad and withdrawn. "You still haven't said what you're going to do."

"Only the one thing I can do," Cash answered. "I gotta wait for Steve to call on me ag'in. And you can be sure he will. I get my chance this next time, I gotta get alone with Ethan and somehow try to talk some sense into him."

"And if he won't listen?" Lucinda's voice became impatient. "Cash, from what you've told me, your brother's already made up his mind. Do you really think you can convince him about Reno?"

Cash sighed. "It's a slim chance, I know. But it's the only one I got."

He wanted Lucinda to get on a stage and ride away from town. But she wouldn't agree. If she couldn't be with him, she at least wanted to be nearby. After more discussion the couple compromised when Cash convinced Lucinda to move herself into a hotel room for a few days. He told her it wouldn't be a long wait. He'd be sure to hear from Steve very soon. If Cash was certain of one thing, it was that Steve Reno didn't want him too far from him.

Lucinda packed a couple of small bags containing only her essentials. She would be checking into the Landmark Hotel, the Dead Eye Molly's of rooming accommodations, set at the edge of town, where dirt-baked cowboys just off the range would stop and where no proper lady would room. But that was why Cash wanted her there. Its male-dominated reputation made the Landmark about the safest place for Lucinda in Wyatt City. Far from the reach of Steve Reno.

She notified her boss at the coffee shop that she'd be away from work for about a week to stay with a sick friend in Laramie. He accepted her story. Cash made it clear that she was not to leave her room until she heard from him. He knew Lucinda would be all right once she got herself settled. She'd proven herself to be a gal who could take care of herself.

There was just one final precaution Cash wanted her to take. He asked her if she owned a gun. She looked puzzled; then a concerned look crossed her face.

"A small derringer," she said.

"Know how to use it?"

"Haven't shot a gun for a while. Used to do some shooting with my brothers when I was in California."

"Loaded?"

She nodded, still a little unsure about the questioning. "Since the day I bought it. About two months ago."

"Look," Cash said. "Leave me with the derringer. I want you to stuff the Colt into one of your bags and take it along with you."

"But—" she started to protest.

"Just do as I say. I'll feel better knowing you're protected. Plus

I think it'd be smart if I carried a gun that wasn't so easily noticed."

Cash walked over to the bureau and handed her the Colt with the four bullets. She accepted it tentatively and told him her pistol was in the top drawer of her bedroom dresser. He went to get it. It was a two-barrel Remington derringer that could easily fit into his pocket without being detected.

Cash stood with her at the door, and they hugged. Lucinda held on to him long and tightly, not wanting to let him go. Cash finally had to break their embrace. He smiled confidently at her. Lucinda looked sad but told him she understood. Cash felt relieved. He needed to hear her say that. It meant that Lucinda had come to see that this temporary separation was best for both of them. Cash didn't want her at risk—and he didn't want to be worrying about her while he waited for his next call from Steve Reno.

Cash didn't doubt for a moment that she would have stayed beside him through all that was to come. He couldn't resist the affection he felt for her any longer, and he kissed her hard. She welcomed it.

Cash couldn't chance stepping out into the open while it was still daylight and so stood inside the doorway when she left. His one worry was that Steve or one of his gang might be keeping watch on the house. He doubted that was the case, but he had told Lucinda to keep watchful until she could get a carriage ride to the hotel. She would recognize Steve or Slug Fletcher, having been in their presence, but wouldn't know Andy Chelsea—or Ethan, for that matter. Her leaving the house alone might be a bit of a gamble, but one that had become necessary.

Cash slightly parted the curtains of the front window and watched her walk slowly up to the main street. He couldn't see anyone around, but that didn't necessarily mean someone was not watching.

He turned away from the window and looked around the parlor. The house seemed empty without Lucinda. All he could do to fill his time until the next call came from Steve was to try to keep himself from thinking troubling thoughts.

Cash had always said that his thoughts were his own worst

enemy and that he was never smart to open himself too much to them. But that's what quickly happened. Despite his efforts, he couldn't seem to relax. While he had sent Lucinda away so that he wouldn't worry about her, Cash *was* worried. He would have no way of knowing whether she reached the hotel safely. Or if Steve or one of his killers had intercepted her, part of another scheme to bind Cash more tightly into his trap. Cash had no idea how Steve Reno's brain worked anymore.

He realized he had to stop tormenting himself. There was nothing he could do . . . and he wouldn't know anything definite until he next heard from Steve.

Yet in an odd way, maybe some good came out of his worrying. He had come to truly recognize his feelings for Lucinda. How much she mattered to him. The private little smile he wore in consideration of this thought soon faded, though, as he concluded that if anything should happen to her, he'd strap on side arms and walk the streets of town until he found Steve Reno and would kill him dead on the spot.

Or maybe Steve would outdraw him. Either way, it really wouldn't matter. Without Lucinda, Cash realized he didn't have much to live for.

As the darkness of night once again encroached over the territory, Cash grew restless and impatient and found himself giving in to nerves. He couldn't seem to marshal his thoughts into any cohesive or constructive pattern. He was on edge, waiting for that knock on the door.

He expected it, yet he feared it, because he couldn't be sure what that knock would bring. Maybe tonight would be when Steve decided he'd played his game long enough. Or maybe Cash would learn something about Lucinda that he didn't want to know. Every slight noise he heard made his heart skip a beat. He sat in the rocker with the derringer resting in his hand. Cash didn't much like guns, but holding that small, two-barreled pistol gave him some comfort.

It was the long waiting that unsettled him most. Although he felt it in his gut that Steve would be calling tonight, he might just postpone his visit to make Cash sweat a little longer. He could do anything he wanted. Since the beginning, he was the one dealing all the cards.

Cash watched as heavy shadows crept into the room until all natural light faded. He lit the kerosene lantern on the table next to him, at the same time igniting the tip of the cigarette he had rolled in the flame. He never moved from the rocker, swaying back and forth with a steady, gentle motion, gun sitting close by on his lap. Soon fatigue set in, and Cash found himself struggling to stay awake until, finally, he surrendered to the heaviness of his eyelids.

It wasn't a restful sleep. All at once it seemed as if he were plunged into terrible nightmares. Fortunately most of what he dreamed would be forgotten. But he would retain two vivid images that he feared would stay with him for a long time. There was Steve Reno in his expensive city-slicker suit, laughing like a mad-man as he stood in a sea of blood littered with hundred-dollar bills . . . and, even more disturbing, the haunting sight of Molly hobbling around with her deformed eye exposed and the black patch covering the empty socket of what had been her good eye. . . .

Cash awoke with a shout and a start. He was bathed in a cold sweat and breathing heavily. Trying to recover from the horror of what he'd dreamed, he sat awake for the rest of the long night.

The next day's sun was bright, and its light penetrated the pat-terned fabric of the drawn curtains, creating white specks of light that danced across the walls. Cash still hadn't moved from the rocker, and his neck and shoulders were a little stiff, so he pivoted his head and rocked his shoulders to loosen up a bit. Then he got up. He could have used a bath but instead pumped water into a basin and gave himself a good wash and shave.

Even as he tried to keep busy with routine tasks, Cash couldn't ease himself of two persistent and troubling thoughts: was Lu-cinda safe . . . and why hadn't Steve come last night?

He'd just finished with the last strokes of the razor when he heard the knocking at the door. The knock he had been expecting—and dreading.

At first he stood perfectly still, unsure if he would even be able to move to answer it. Then came another round of knocking, and

Cash got to thinking that if it was Steve or one of his boys, why would they come calling so early, during the day? That wasn't the pattern Steve had established. They'd kept their visits nocturnal.

Cash considered not answering the door, just let whoever was there think no one was home. But he had to find out. He wiped the last bit of shaving soap from his face and went into the parlor to fetch the derringer off the coffee table where he'd left it. He then crept over to the door and parted the curtain draped over the side glass just a little.

Standing out on the porch was Garrett O'Dowd. *Sheriff* O'Dowd.

Cash stepped back quickly, hoping the sheriff hadn't noticed the faint shifting of the curtain. Garrett would have no business showing up here . . . unless in his desperation to find Cash he'd started going house-to-house. But that wasn't very likely. No . . . it was more likely that someone had told him Cash was hiding out at the house. And that someone would either have to be Steve . . . or Lucinda.

Cash stood away from the door, gripping the derringer and trying to keep his breathing steady. If Garrett tried to break into the house, Cash wasn't sure what he would do. And if the sheriff knew for a certainty that he was inside, Cash expected him to do just that.

But instead Cash heard his voice call out, "McCall, I know you're in there. I want to have a word with you."

Instinctively, Cash clicked back the hammer on the derringer. He now made the decision that if Garrett came through that door, he *would* kill him. What did he have to lose? He was as much a dead man anyway.

Cash heard him fiddling with the knob, rattling and tugging at it. Knocking at the door with more urgency.

Then again his voice. "McCall, if you can hear me, I want you to let me in. I won't be drawin' my gun. But what I gotta say is important—to both of us."

He was making it sound as if Cash could trust him. Or was he just speaking those words to get him to open the door? Cash could continue to ignore him, and he might go away. But he'd be sure to be back later. And then he might not come alone or be as friendly as he sounded now.

Or Cash could let him into the house—but on his terms.

There was also the slim possibility that Garrett might be bluffing, playing a hunch that Cash was at the house. Grabbing at the few straws he had left. But how was Cash to know?

Cash didn't know what the hell to do. He couldn't see himself coming out ahead no matter what his decision.

For the longest time there was just quiet. The knocking stopped. No twisting of the knob. No more talking. Cash stood perfectly still. Then he heard Garrett's boots as they clomped down the porch steps. Once the sound faded, Cash ventured back to the side window and glanced outside through the curtain.

The sheriff looked to be gone.

But Cash couldn't afford to let himself grow too relaxed. There was every chance he would be back. Maybe sooner. Maybe later. Either way, Cash couldn't risk staying in the house. Because Garrett at the very least *suspected* Cash might be there, he had to get out. He started to wonder if maybe he'd made a mistake not hearing what he had to say. But he convinced himself it had most likely been a trick.

Cash had one hell of a problem. He would have to leave the house in broad daylight. Try to get somewhere without half the town noticing him. And how did he know Garrett didn't have some deputies in hiding around the place, just waiting for him to step outside?

While he stood there, lost in the confusion of his thoughts, trying to decide if he had any option left open, Cash heard footfalls come up from behind him. He stood glued to his spot, not daring to turn around, as he realized he had just run out of options.

He heard Garrett's voice, speaking softly. "Locks in these old houses ain't too difficult to open."

Cash slowly turned his head. Garrett was facing him, though Cash was surprised to see that his gun was holstered.

"No need for gunplay," Garrett explained in a calm voice. "And I'd suggest you put away your pistol too. As I said, just come to talk."

"Lemme hear what you have to say first," Cash said, working to keep his voice controlled as he raised the derringer toward the sheriff with his finger firmly on the trigger.

Cash wasn't about to surrender his leverage.

Garrett squinted, clearly displeased at having to talk into the barrel of a gun. But he drew a breath and nodded.

"Mind if I sit?" he said.

Cash flickered his eyes toward the two seating arrangements in the parlor.

"Go ahead," he said. "But if'n you don't mind, I'll stay standin'."

Garrett shrugged and took a seat on the sofa. He glanced about the room.

"Nice house," he commented. "Comfortable. Remember some years back when it used to be *real* comfortable."

Cash wasn't in the mood for small talk. "You got somethin' to be tellin' me, just get on with it."

"All right. Your girl, Lucinda, came by the office to see me," Garrett began.

Cash felt relief that Lucinda was safe. At the same time he experienced a cold rush of resentment that she had gone to the sheriff against his word.

Garrett could see the anger tightening Cash's expression and spoke up quickly. "Now hold on, McCall," he said with a raised hand. "Whether you know it or not, she done you a favor." He took a breath. "She told me what happened—at least your side of it. Fact is, I don't think you'd be lyin' to her."

"What exactly did she tell you?" Cash asked.

"'Bout the Wells Fargo holdup. What you said happened there. And that Steve Reno tried to pin the whole affair on you and Chick McGraw."

Cash didn't say anything. He wanted to hear more.

Garrett wore a slight smile. "Look, I grew up with you boys. I know you ain't much good, but I never pictured you for a killer. Steve Reno's a different matter. He's a tinhorn desperado. Even as a kid I saw him as a bad specimen headed for big trouble. So what you say happened ain't somethin' I have a problem acceptin'. Yep, just hadda hear the name Steve Reno to start fittin' the pieces together."

"Yeah?"

Garrett nodded. "Also, thanks to what your girl provided me, I notified the Federal marshal to check on that stolen gold shipment in Laramie. Once that's uncovered, I guarantee you Reno and his gang won't be looked upon too favorably by whoever it is they're workin' for." He paused, then spoke quietly. "And I know 'bout your brother, Ethan, bein' in with Reno. I think that if we work together, we might set this right. To both our benefit."

Cash regarded Garrett suspiciously. "Work together?"

Garrett spoke straight. "I need you, and if you're smart, you'll see that you need me. You don't wanna hang for killin's you ain't responsible for."

"So . . . where would that leave me?" Cash asked cautiously.

"You ain't gonna walk away scot-free, McCall. Reckon you know that. But if you agree to help me get Reno and them others, I'll do whatever I can to see that the court goes easy on you. You have my word."

"I've trusted too many people's word," Cash remarked with a sneer.

"The *wrong* people, McCall," Garrett said solidly.

He had a point. Cash couldn't argue with him there.

Garrett spoke the facts. "Don't you think it woulda been easier for me to come up behind you just now with a gun in my hand? I could be marchin' you off to jail right as we speak. You'd take full blame for the robbery *and* them killin's, and no one would be the wiser, 'cause no one would know no different. Look pretty good on me too. But I'm willin' to trust you on this, and I need you to be trustin' me."

"Where's Lucinda now?" Cash asked him.

"Wherever you sent her," Garrett answered with a shrug. "She wouldn't say, and I didn't ask. She told me you don't want her involved."

"I don't."

"Then that's fine with me."

The derringer began to ease in Cash's grip. Maybe Garrett and he were on opposite sides of the fence, but Cash couldn't deny he was playing fair. It would still be a dangerous game with Reno, especially the way Cash was planning to proceed. But he did feel some of his burden being lifted.

The problem was that even with Garrett and him siding together, Cash still had to go it alone against Steve Reno.

He stepped over to the rocker and sat. "You got a plan?" he asked.

"Not so much a plan," Garrett said, crinkling his brow. "I just need what you can tell me. 'Bout who's in Steve's gang and where they're hidin' out."

Cash nodded, and his lips curled in a smile. "Only three things wrong with what you're askin' me, Garrett. One: once I tell you who's in with Steve and where they are—that's if'n I know—you got no reason not to have me arrested. Not sayin' I don't trust you, but what more use would I be to you? Second: you and your deputies go in after 'em, and I guarantee there's gonna be shootin'. I gotta try and get my brother away 'fore that happens. Third, Garrett: I got a personal score to settle with Reno."

Garrett squinted his eyes. "You plannin' to kill him yourself?"

"Can't be sure the court'll judge him fairly," Cash said, adding tightly, "By that I mean seein' him dancin' off the end of a rope."

Garrett spoke abruptly. "Molly Ferguson's body was found 'bout a mile off the main road yesterday."

Cash lowered his eyes but made no comment.

"She was shot 'tween the eyes." Garrett paused to look at Cash. "Know anything 'bout it?"

"No," Cash said, responding not too quickly and not too slowly. He wanted his single utterance to sound convincing.

All the same, Garrett looked a shade doubtful.

Cash swiftly changed the topic. "I'll bargain with you, Garrett. I'll do what I can to find where Steve's at. But once I do, I first gotta talk to Ethan. You gotta guarantee me there won't be no interference or no tricks. Once I know my brother is safe, and if I'm able to walk out alive . . . I'll get back to you and let you know where they are."

"What 'bout your grudge with Reno?" Garrett wanted to know. "Can't condone no cold-blooded murder, even if it's ag'in an outlaw rat like that."

Cash spoke thoughtfully. "Reckon we'll play that as it comes. Can't give you my word, Garrett, 'cause I can't be sure what Steve has in mind. It might come down to him or me, and I aim to be lookin' out for myself."

"Might be you're hopin' for that outcome," Garrett conjectured with a straight expression.

"Might be."

"All right. Sounds 'bout as fair as we can go, McCall."

"Best you'll get from me," Cash returned.

"But I can't be waitin' long," Garrett added with a stiff pointing of his finger.

Cash nodded, then said, "In the meantime I gotta have your word I won't have no trouble."

"Not from my people, McCall. But I wouldn't advise you to be makin' yourself too visible on the streets. We ain't taken down that reward poster yet."

"Dead or alive," Cash mused without humor.

Chapter Sixteen

Cash now had an unexpected and unofficial partner. He couldn't say unwanted, though. While he still didn't know if he could completely trust Garrett, he felt pretty confident of his intentions after their talk.

Either way it made no difference as far as Cash's dealings with Steve Reno were concerned. At the first opportunity Steve was a dead man, and Cash wouldn't be waiting to shoot him in self-defense, either.

The five-thousand-dollar bounty on his head still worried Cash, since he knew the *Dead* in the *Dead or Alive* posting could be collected by any eager citizen with a gun, without consideration for the self-defense Garrett expected Cash to observe with Steve Reno.

But Cash wouldn't be out roaming the streets looking for Steve, and he felt sure he wouldn't have to. Wherever Steve might be at the moment, Cash expected him to come by. He wasn't about to leave a loose end.

And just around dusk Cash got his visit.

A heavy knocking at the door. Cash was sitting in the parlor having a drink when it sounded, loud enough to give him a start. He rose from the rocker and hastened to pocket the derringer that he'd kept close to him. Then he walked to the door.

He glanced out the side window and saw Slug Fletcher standing alone on the porch, clad in a duster with his hands thrust deeply into the pockets. Pulling in a breath, Cash opened the door.

Slug said nothing, and neither did Cash. There was no need for words. Cash just grabbed his Stetson and followed Slug outside.

Tonight they had a new destination but one that Cash was not unfamiliar with. It was the secluded cabin hideout Steve had chosen for the Wells Fargo robbery. The buggy ride was long, and Cash felt nervous and uncomfortable the whole trip. If this was the night Steve planned to square accounts, he'd picked a perfect spot.

The moon was out, but the skies were starting to cloud over. The night air was cool, and a slight feel of dampness foretold a later rain. Cash could define the shadowy outlines of the mountain crests far in the distance. The road was silent, though a slight breeze occasionally rustled through the tree branches. The only other sound Cash recognized was the occasional scurrying of small animals in the brush.

They didn't ride the buggy the whole way. Upon the trail they stopped when they came to two horses tied to a couple of trees. Slug climbed out of the buggy and waited for Cash to follow. Some shadowy figure Cash couldn't recognize stepped forward from where the horses were and, wordlessly, got in and turned the buggy around back toward town. Since he wouldn't be riding back to Wyatt in the backseat protection of the buggy, Cash quickly concluded that it was Steve's intention he wouldn't be riding back at all.

Before Cash could get up on his mount, Slug came up behind him and pressed his revolver into his back. Cash slowly turned to him. Slug's expression was vacant, but the threat of his person hung dark and heavy, like the rain clouds that had formed in the sky.

"Ride slow," was all he said.

That was all Cash could do once they started down the dark trail. As they rode, Slug kept close behind, Colt aimed steady at Cash's back.

A dim light emanated from the cabin that Cash could spot from the road. He carefully directed his horse down the narrow sloping trail leading toward it, ever aware of the clip-clopping of Slug's mount following him.

There were three horses tied to a weathered old hitching post outside the cabin, and Cash knew whom they belonged to. One likely had been ridden by Ethan, whom Cash hoped was among those waiting inside the cabin.

Slug and Cash looped the reins of their horses around the post, only Cash purposely kept his own loose. Then Slug gestured him forward.

With his heart starting to beat heavily in his chest, Cash opened the door and walked inside.

Steve and Andy Chelsea were seated quietly at the table. The first thing Cash noticed was how Steve wasn't dressed in his fancy city clothes. He was in plain cowboy wear: pale blue shirt, brown pants, leather vest, red kerchief knotted 'round his neck. Cash saw that there was a bottle on the table. Steve had a glass of whiskey in his hand. Andy didn't.

Cash didn't see Ethan.

The Indian glared at him, but Steve grinned with what looked like genuine pleasure when he saw Cash standing in the doorway.

"Compadre," he greeted briskly. "Come on over and take a seat."

"Why are we meetin' here?" Cash said cautiously, though the question didn't need answering.

Steve opened the palms of his hands. "Thought it smart to keep outta town for a bit. Now that O'Dowd's back . . . and after that little incident at Dead Eye's. 'Spose you heard they found her."

Cash nodded. "I heard."

Steve took a swallow of his whiskey, smacking his lips at the taste.

"Not like you, Steve," Cash remarked, adding with a sly edge, "You was always good at coverin' your tracks."

Steve got his meaning. "Yeah," was all he said.

Cash's eyes narrowed questioningly. "I saw three horses outside. But there's just the two of you."

"Your brother?" Steve said harmlessly. He jerked a thumb toward a partially opened door through which a faint shaft of light emerged. "He's in the next room, sacked out."

Cash frowned and started to move toward the door. Steve stood up fast and said, "You can see him in a minute, Cash. First we gotta have us a talk."

Cash halted, because he couldn't do anything else. Not with the Indian and Slug Fletcher staring at him with death in their eyes. He stepped to the table and sat down, and Steve did likewise. The shadow of Slug hovered over Cash's shoulders.

He waited for Steve to speak, and Reno took his time. All Cash could hear during those moments was Slug's heavy wheezing behind him.

A sudden gust of wind rattled the window glass, and Cash, already unnerved, reacted with a start. Steve, ever watchful, noticed and smiled thinly.

Finally he said, "Reckon you already figgered why I sent for you tonight." The tone of his voice held no portent of threat; he was speaking matter-of-factly.

"I figgered."

"And knowin' that, you didn't come heeled?" Steve said, taking note that Cash wore no gun belt.

Cash shook his head slowly. "Couldn't see no point. 'Sides, that bullet you put into me kinda stiffened up my gun hand."

That was true. His right hand, the hand he favored for shooting, was not one he could depend on now, though Cash quickly regretted admitting that to Steve.

"Well, that's mighty obligin'." Steve exhaled a slow breath that sounded almost regretful. "Hadda be this way, compadre," he explained. "Too bad." He busily scratched the back of his head. "Y'know, Cash, woulda been easier all 'round if you'd been killed back at Taylor's Pass. Guess I never was much of a shot."

"Thought 'bout that a lot and could never rightly figger if you intended me dead."

"Can't be sure of that myself," Steve said musingly.

"And what 'bout Laramie? Your partners?"

"Told you before, it was their plan," Steve said. "I hadda go along with it. I got a big future with them boys."

Steve obviously hadn't learned that the Federal marshal was in Laramie as they spoke, tracking down the gold shipment. As Garrett O'Dowd had told him, once the gold was found, that would pretty much finish Steve's "future" with his partners.

Cash kept the conversation going. "So all what you said 'bout us workin' together was . . . just talk."

"You ain't a part of it," Steve said flatly.

"Reckon I knew that." Cash looked out the window and saw the full glow of the moon, some of its light spilling through the glass. He turned back to Steve and leaned forward. He spoke his next words with conviction.

"Steve, maybe I got what was comin' to me. I put myself into this—got no one to blame but myself. But my brother ain't guilty of nothin'—'cept maybe lookin' up to you and takin' you at your word. Kill me if you're gonna. But give the kid a break."

Steve leaned back in his chair and clasped his hands behind his head as his face took on a contemplative expression. It looked as if he were seriously considering what Cash was asking. He then sat forward and rubbed the palm of his hand over his stubbled chin.

Cash waited. He didn't dare speak further. He'd made his point, and no amount of begging or pleading would change the decision Steve would make.

Steve then pushed his chair back and got to his feet. Cash noticed how he gestured slightly with his eyes for Slug to go into the room where he'd said Ethan was asleep. Cash started to rise as he feared the worst was about to happen. Steve smiled at him, nodding his head toward the door.

"C'mon, Cash," he said in a friendly voice. "Your brother's waitin' to see you."

Still uncertain, Cash walked toward the room with Steve leading the way. Steve stopped in front of the open doorway so that Cash couldn't see all the way into the room. Then, with a smile, he stepped aside. Though the lantern light was dim, Cash instantly caught a sight he'd never hoped to see.

His brother, Ethan, beaten and bloody and bound with rawhide to a chair.

And Slug Fletcher was standing next to him with his Colt pressed against his skull.

Chapter Seventeen

In the next instant, before Cash could even think to react, his arms were pinned behind his back by Andy Chelsea, who'd crept up on him like the skilled redskin he was and who held fast. He wasn't a big man, but he was powerful, and Cash's struggles against his sturdy grip were futile. He finally surrendered.

All Cash could do was stand there, eyes focused on his brother.

Ethan looked to be in terrible shape. Slug Fletcher, the onetime professional bare-knuckle fighter, had given him a thorough working over. He'd beaten him throughout the day, at intervals, so not to kill him outright, which any of Slug's powerful punches could have done, leaving Ethan helpless and bound to the chair. Ethan's eyes were black and swollen, and his nose had been busted again. Cash's so-handsome-he-was-pretty brother now had a face that was hardly recognizable. He was barely conscious, his head lolling drunkenly and his bloodshot eyes rolled back in their sockets.

When his eyes seemed to regain their focus, Ethan fixed them squarely upon Cash. They widened in recognition and were pleading.

"Let him go, Steve," Cash said, the words leaving his mouth as numb as his comprehension of the terrible sight.

Steve ignored him and stepped past Cash into the room and over to the chair. As he looked at Ethan, he gave his head a slow, regretful shake.

"It's real unfortunate, compadre," he said to Cash. "Like I told you, the kid had promise. 'Fact, it was Ethan here who took care of our little problem with ol' Dead Eye."

165

Molly?

Cash didn't know what his face was expressing, but his brain could neither grasp nor accept what he was hearing.

No, he thought feverishly. *It isn't true. Ethan's just a kid. My brother. He's not a killer!*

Steve was lying like the treacherous snake he was. Trying to keep him at odds with the kid, even as he prepared to kill the both of them. He wanted Ethan to die thinking his brother despised him.

Which, dammit—for their mother, for Molly, for permitting himself to fall under Steve's spell of lies—Cash had to confess, he almost did.

He could feel the blood drain from his face until he was sure he had the deathly pallor of a corpse.

"Yeah," Steve said, impressed at the memory. "He put one right 'tween her eyes. Didn't so much as flinch when he pulled the trigger."

Cash spoke desperately. "It's not him you want, Steve. It's me."

Steve's face turned toward him, and his voice was intense. "And maybe that woulda been the way. Only . . . I got word you had some company this afternoon. Our old pal O'Dowd. *Sheriff* O'Dowd."

Cash felt his body stiffen. Then he made himself recover, and as calmly as he possibly could he explained the situation, lying to clear himself.

"Yeah. He showed up," Cash told him. "Snuck up on me, in fact. But I didn't tell him nothin'. You think I'd chance—"

"Ain't what I think," Steve said, interrupting him. "It's what I know. And I know that you talked, compadre. You spilled the beans 'bout everythin'."

Cash was stunned. There was no way Steve could have known what Garrett and he had talked about. And it hadn't been Cash who'd given the details of the stagecoach robbery to Garrett. It was Lucinda, who'd spoken to the sheriff earlier. The only way Steve could have learned this was from one of the sheriff's own men.

Or . . . maybe from Garrett himself.

Steve wouldn't say how he'd found out about the visit, and Cash reckoned at this point it didn't really matter.

Steve took the revolver from Slug and opened the cylinder, examining it. Cash watched uncomprehendingly as Steve emptied out the bullets, reinserting just one cartridge before snapping the cylinder closed and giving it a spin. He handed the Colt back to Slug.

He turned his eyes toward Cash. "You want I should give the kid a chance?" he said. "Okay, compadre, here it is. One bullet. Six chambers. Three tries. Fifty-fifty odds. This way at least one of you stands a chance of walkin' out alive."

Cash couldn't be tricked. But he kept his voice strong. "You know damn well neither of us is gonna leave here alive."

"You really wanna call me on that?" Steve challenged defiantly.

Cash then shouted out of outrage and his utter helplessness, "If you're gonna kill him, for God's sake just do it! No need for this."

"I'd rather make it a game, compadre," Steve said in a taunt. "You know I've always liked games of chance."

"Everything with you's been a game," Cash said scornfully.

"That's right, friend," Steve agreed. "And every game comes to an end . . . and every game has a winner."

Cash heard a sharp moan come from his brother.

Steve turned to Slug and gave him an unhurried nod.

At once deadpan, Slug Fletcher jammed the barrel of the revolver against the side of Ethan's head. The kid flinched at the impact.

Cash cringed, fighting back the urge to go for the derringer secreted in his pants pocket. But the small gun only held two shots, and there were three outlaws, including Andy Chelsea, standing behind him, who, though he had let go of his arms, Cash could sense was hoping he'd try some impulsive move. He was holding an object, pointed and sharp, against Cash's back, periodically giving a slight jab, like a reminder.

Ethan had enough awareness about him to begin to struggle against the rawhide binding him to the chair.

And all Cash could do was stand there, frustrated in his

helplessness, his jaw clenched, tears clouding his eyes. Holding on to a vain hope that Steve would honor his word . . . if his brother survived his "game."

Ethan tried to speak, but only incoherent sounds escaped his lips. He feebly pivoted his head against the barrel of the gun until Slug grabbed him by the hair and held his head steady.

Cash dropped his eyes to the floor before Slug tugged at the trigger.

Click.

"One," Steve began counting.

Cash tossed a stupidly hopeful look to his brother as Slug lifted the gun to inspect it, then again pressed the barrel tightly against Ethan's skull.

He pulled the trigger a second time.

Click.

Once more Cash had lowered his eyes. He looked up and pushed out an involuntary breath.

"That's two," Steve said, unnecessarily.

Though Cash knew it was doubtful, he held on to the desperate hope that maybe his brother had a chance. If the hammer next hit on an empty chamber, maybe Steve would be satisfied and abide by the rules of his "game." And if he did, Cash would do everything he could to convince Steve that Ethan would never talk against him—not without putting his own neck into a noose for murdering Molly. Cash would get Ethan to promise that he'd ride fast, off into another state, where they'd never hear from him again.

He only prayed that he'd have the chance to convince him after that next pull of the trigger. . . .

Steve regarded Cash with a vague expression. "Last shot. All or nothing, compadre."

Then Slug looked at him with his ugly, grim face. A thin smile creased his fat, wet lips as he pushed the gun against Ethan's head one last time.

Cash made the decision in those final seconds that if that shot killed his brother, he would make the move that would surely earn him a bullet or a blade in the back from Andy Chelsea. Even though he could not depend on his strength or accuracy, given the stiffness in the fingers of his gun hand, as carefully as he could with the Indian standing behind him, Cash slowly and unobtrusively started to slide his hand downward toward his pocket.

Slug pulled the trigger.

Click.

Cash's heart seemed to have stopped at the harmless sound. Again he exhaled a heavy breath.

The cabin fell quiet.

Slug then snapped open the cylinder and lifted the revolver, giving it a shake. No bullet dropped out.

All the time the gun had been empty.

"Palmed the bullet," Steve confessed, smiling from the teeth out as he studied the anxious look on Cash's face. He opened his hand to show him the cartridge.

Cash couldn't find his voice, though his features darkened with hostility.

"Game over, compadre," Steve said. He added darkly, "And I'm a sore loser."

Time stood still only for an instant. And then all hell broke loose.

In one swift, fluid move Steve had his fancy silver-mounted, pearl-handled Colt .45 drawn, and he fired a single shot clean through Ethan's heart. The kid's body jerked backward, tilting the front legs of the chair; then his head dropped lifelessly to his chest.

Ethan McCall died without making a sound.

Cash's shout of protest never escaped his lips, lodging in his throat at the moment the bullet tore through his brother.

Reacting purely on survival instinct, Cash thrust his elbow back as hard as he could and rammed it into Andy's gut, catching him by surprise and doubling him over with a groan. By now Steve had his gun turned toward Cash, who flung himself aside just as Reno let off a shot. The bullet passed close enough that Cash heard it whiz by his ear.

Slug was unarmed, since his Colt had been emptied of bullets, and he moved his bulk, which provided an easy target, off to the

side of the room, out of the line of gunfire. Cash gripped the derringer firmly in his stiffened hand and quickly fired the only two
bullets his pistol held at Steve, causing him to also duck for cover.
Cash then gave the crouched-over Andy a hard kick to the belly
that sent him sprawling onto his back, and rushed out the door toward the hitching rail where he'd loosely secured his horse in an-
ticipation of a fast getaway. He whipped the animal into a dead
run, racing up the treacherous trail onto the main road and back
into Wyatt City.

Chapter Eightteen

He couldn't go back to the house. That was the first place they'd look, and Cash was sure they would soon be following. He'd have to join up with Lucinda at the Landmark Hotel. The thing was, he couldn't be sure how safe he'd be there; Steve seemed to anticipate his every move.

Cash didn't know how soon Steve and his boys would arrive. So he made the decision to get to Lucinda first before going to Garrett O'Dowd. Although he still had a faint doubt about the sheriff—wasn't sure if he could entirely trust him and was even considering the disturbing possibility that O'Dowd may have provided the information to Steve Reno—he had little choice under the circumstances but to play his one potential high card all the way.

He leaped off the horse in front of the hotel and let it run loose down the street. He couldn't chance the gang tracking him to the hotel by recognizing the lone animal standing outside. Then he hurried inside the building. The lobby was dark and empty except for the desk clerk, a plump, balding man wearing horn-rimmed glasses, looking bored at this late hour behind the counter. Cash had to consider that he might recognize him, though with the types of people the hotel serviced, Cash probably looked no better or worse than any of them. He crossed to the counter and asked for Lucinda Gee's room number. The clerk looked at Cash with only a moment's suspicion, eyes squinting behind the thick lenses of his spectacles, then with an elaborate gesture wet his thumb and started flipping through the ledger.

Cash didn't have time for that and grabbed the book from him. "She only checked in a coupla days ago," he grumbled impatiently.

"You ain't doin' that much business not to know a lady come here."

"Oh," the clerk said, pretending to suddenly remember. "Yes, a lady did check in two days ago. Name's not Gee, though."

"What name did she give?" Cash asked, suddenly impressed at Lucinda's efficiency.

The clerk thought for a moment. "Morris, I believe," he said. "Yes, Barbara Morris."

"What room?"

"Is she expecting you?"

"Just gimme the room number," Cash snapped.

The clerk reluctantly obliged. "Three-o-four."

Cash gave the clerk a hard look, then bounded up the corner stairs to the third floor. He knocked lightly on the door and soon heard footfalls approaching from inside.

"It's me. Cash," he said before she could ask.

The door was quickly unlocked, and Lucinda let him in. The first thing Cash noticed was how rough she looked. The stress she'd been living with was evident in the lines that now stretched across her face. But she was relieved and happy to see him, and they hugged. Cash appreciated her affection but finally had to ease her aside. He asked if she had a drink. She said she didn't have anything but that she could pick up a bottle from the saloon just down the street. Cash didn't want either one of them out on the street with Steve and his bunch sure to soon be riding into town, and he suggested she give the desk clerk a couple of bucks to run over to the saloon and fetch them some whiskey. Once she went downstairs, Cash allowed himself a moment to flop onto the bed and try to sort out his thoughts. But now that he could afford a stop from the fever-rush of the past few hours, the only thing his brain seemed capable of processing was a replaying of the horrible events. The images of what happened at the cabin—to Ethan—were burned into his memory.

When Lucinda returned with the whiskey the clerk had agreed to buy for her, she and Cash sat together on the edge of the bed, and they both had a stiff drink in silence. Then Cash had a little more. Lucinda was patient and didn't press for the story. She waited until Cash appeared more composed and ready to tell her what happened.

The events were too fresh, and it was a painful reliving.

"I'm so sorry about your brother," she said compassionately after Cash finished.

Cash felt tired and defeated. "He chose his own road," he said. "Once he got in with Reno, he never had a chance."

Yeah, Cash thought heavily, his brother was dead. There was nothing he could do about that. And he couldn't hold himself responsible. It might be difficult, maybe even impossible, but he had to try to rid himself of all the guilt he'd been carrying, because it was Ethan who'd made the choice. Maybe Cash could be blamed for failing him as a brother, but Ethan was no longer a boy and should have been smart enough to know right from wrong. He'd wanted to be an outlaw. Nothing Cash could have done would have changed that.

Lucinda spoke with her own gratitude. "But you're alive, Cash. Thank God."

He gave her a gentle smile. He didn't want to puncture her optimism by adding what he was thinking: *but for how long?*

He said, "You'd better hand me that revolver I gave you."

Lucinda put her glass down and retrieved the gun from one of her bags. She sat back beside him on the bed, and while Cash held the Colt, she took a sip of her drink and spoke in an apologetic tone.

"I went to the sheriff," she said.

Cash rocked his head without looking at her. "I know."

"I know you told me not to, but I was so afraid, and—" she started to say.

"It's all right," Cash assured her, patting her hand. "Probably a smart move."

The hard liquor and the day's excitement made Cash suddenly sleepy. But he knew he had to fight it. He couldn't count on Steve not tracking him right to this room. He had to keep awake until morning, when, if things stayed quiet, he would risk going through town to report to Garrett. He doubted he had the energy to make the short trip now and felt they should be safe in their room till sunup.

"Cash," Lucinda said softly. "What are we going to do?"

He reached over and laid the six-shooter on the nightstand. He didn't answer right away. Partly because he didn't know. And partly . . . because if he had a future left to him, he had to consider sharing it with Lucinda. This gal had stayed by him through his whole terrible ordeal, and Cash had hardly given any thought to her loyalty and, he reckoned, her love, so consumed had he been with revenge and with rescuing his brother from the clutches of The Whiskey Kid.

But he would have to give her an answer to her question.

It was one Cash wasn't sure she'd want to hear.

"Even if we fix this with Reno, I'll probably have to do jail time. Reckon I'm okay with that. I have it comin'. Garrett says he'll put in a word for me; the courts might go easy. Could be for the best."

Her response surprised Cash.

"It would be," Lucinda said eagerly. "You'd be free afterward, and we could start a new life together." She lowered her eyes, maybe thinking she'd spoken too fast. Or said too much. "If . . . you'd want me with you."

Cash turned to her and smiled. "You think I'd want it any other way?"

Lucinda looked relieved. So much that she leaned toward Cash and pressed her lips against his. He lowered his drink onto the floor and brushed her long black hair away from her face. He wrapped his arms around her small waist and pulled her close. They shared the most honest kiss that Cash had given since they'd met. To Cash, it felt damn good.

When their lips finally separated but with their eyes still locked on one another, Cash breathed a heavy sigh. He felt it was time to give the apology he felt he owed her.

"I'm sorry you've had to go through all this. Wasn't fair that you should be a part—"

Lucinda interrupted. "No," she said, strength and firmness in her voice. "It'll have been worth it. As long as we're together and . . . once it's over, we can put it behind us."

"It's what I want," Cash said, and he spoke those words truthfully.

Lucinda squeezed his hand and continued to reach into his eyes with her loving, supportive gaze.

It was strange, but for those few moments, sitting beside Lucinda in the lamplit gloom of a cheap hotel room, no matter what might be waiting for him outside, Cash's world seemed perfect.

They kissed again, and this time their bodies eased onto the mattress. Cash wanted her close. His emotions had reached a fever boil, and he suddenly needed to give vent to all that was churning around inside of him. Lucinda seemed to understand, and the expression on her face told Cash she was willing. But Cash demurred and fought back the urge. Things were different between them now. Cash loved her, but he also had a respect for her, and he didn't want to use her that way.

The rain that Cash had seen coming when riding out with Slug to the cabin had started to fall, pattering against the window of their room. Strangely it reminded Cash of the rain he and Steve had listened to for days on end during their stay at the canyon cabin following the bank heist in Hensford. A time that now seemed to exist as a distant memory of a faded friendship.

There was a sharp rapping at the door.

Lucinda and Cash pulled apart, and they both sat up abruptly. They faced each other, their expressions marked with apprehension.

"Cash," Lucinda muttered breathlessly, her face suddenly fearful.

Cash had his own reaction. His breath caught in his throat. He swallowed hard to relieve the pressure and so not to surrender to the anxiety that had taken hold. He slowly lifted his body from the side of the bed.

Lucinda grabbed his arm, and her grip was strong. "No," she whispered, her voice tinged with trepidation. "Don't answer it."

But Cash knew better. "Whoever it is won't go away," he said.

"*He* wouldn't know you're here."

Cash didn't answer. Instead he gently removed her hand from his forearm and started toward the door. He halted. His eyes shifted toward the nightstand where he'd laid the .44 Colt. Cash looked back at Lucinda, who was sitting ramrod straight; then he went for the revolver. His gripping it didn't make Lucinda look any more reassured. Nor did Cash feel particularly protected. He took a breath and stepped forward.

That was when Lucinda suddenly jumped up and positioned her body in front of his, blocking his way to the door and raising both her hands to his chest to halt him. She gave Cash a wary look that indicated to him that she should be the one to answer the knock. Cash wasn't quick to agree. He didn't know who was on the other side of the door and sure as hell wasn't eager for either of them to find out. But he finally decided that if it was the trouble he was expecting, her going to the door might give him the chance to ready his move.

Cash nodded and told her very quietly to first ask who was there—and if there was no reply, not to unlock the door but to get out of the way. Fast.

She nodded her head in return, slowly, and just as slowly stepped to the door.

"Yes, who is it?" she said.

Cash was watching closely and noticed how she had the open fingers of her hand pressed tightly against the door frame.

"Desk clerk," the voice on the other side replied.

Lucinda and Cash instantly exchanged relieved looks. But both were cautiously curious what the desk clerk would want at such a late hour, as it was now after midnight.

"Okay, open it," Cash told her, tucking the revolver into the rear waistband of his pants, where he could still reach for it if necessary.

Lucinda unlocked and opened the door. The desk clerk entered, and he was alone. Cash relaxed, though he noticed how the man regarded him with an intense look.

Cash understood in a moment. The clerk's message was for him—one that he didn't want to hear.

"There's some men wantin' to see you. Downstairs in the lobby."

Cash turned to Lucinda. Her mouth was agape, and she looked suddenly unsteady on her feet, almost as if she were about to faint. She leaned her body against Cash's for support, and he wrapped an arm around her shoulders.

"How many men?" Cash asked weakly, over a dry swallow.

"Three," the desk clerk answered. "Said they're friends of yours."

Cash spoke urgently. "Look, friend, those men ain't friends of mine. 'Fact, they've come lookin' for trouble. If you don't wanna see your hotel turned into a shootin' gallery, I'd advise you to get yourself to the sheriff, pronto. You'll find him at his office. He rooms there." He paused. "You got a back way outta here?"

The desk clerk nodded nervously.

"Then you better hurry."

The desk clerk nodded again and rushed off down the hallway. Cash lightly closed the door and leaned back against it, looking at Lucinda, who had dropped onto the room's one chair. Her brown, catlike eyes were wide, and she was trembling.

Steve, Slug, and Andy. They'd tracked him, and much sooner than Cash had expected. He didn't know how they'd found him, though he really wasn't surprised. Steve had been one step ahead of him right from the start.

Of course it didn't really matter *how* they'd found him. The fact was, they had.

Lucinda was wringing her hands. "It's them, isn't it?"

Cash just looked at her without saying anything.

Lucinda's voice became excited. "Cash, you've gotta get away. Use that back way out."

"I'm not leaving you alone with them," Cash said.

He removed the Colt from his waistband and walked it over to the table, laying it gently on the surface. For the moment he couldn't hold it, since his palms had gotten wet with sweat. He tried to rub his hands dry against his pants.

He stared at Lucinda for a long while before he said with resignation, "It has to end."

"Maybe the sheriff will get here and—" she started to say.

"Or maybe they'll just bust in here with their guns blazing," Cash countered. "I don't wanna see you hurt. No, I gotta go down to them."

Lucinda leaped up from the chair and rushed into his arms. Her long raven hair had spilled over her face, but Cash could hear her sobbing and feel her body shuddering. She begged him not to go.

Cash would have given anything in the world to have obliged her. But he knew Steve would not stay patient for long. And if he'd come to kill him, as Cash knew he had, he wouldn't be leaving Lucinda behind. Cash had seen firsthand how he dealt with witnesses.

Cash continued to hold Lucinda close, and in those seconds he thought it ironic how his brief respite with Lucinda had almost taken from him all the hatred he felt for Steve Reno. And now, in facing Steve and his gunmen, he understood that hate would be the most potent weapon he had.

He considered only for an instant how the Fates had allowed him this momentary interlude but had now determined that he could not run.

He gently tilted Lucinda's head upward. He looked directly into her eyes, and she met his gaze. Cash hoped the tender look in his eyes confirmed for Lucinda the love he felt for her. He managed a smile . . .

. . . before he swiftly drew back his fist and punched her solidly in the jaw. Her eyes widened with surprise, then fell upon Cash sadly before they fluttered shut and her body crumpled forward in his one-armed grip, limply, like a rag doll.

Cash held her for only a moment longer before he gently laid her on the floor.

It was what he had to do, Cash justified. The only way he could think of to save Lucinda. But he regretted hitting her, and he had to compose himself for a few moments.

He went to the chair to sit. He wanted to smoke one last cigarette while he readied himself as best he could for what was to come.

Chapter Nineteen

The mist of memories evaporated, and Cash McCall was back in the present. He was climbing down the staircase in the hotel, a paint-chipped outer wall on one side, a wood-paneled partition on the other. He was heading for the lobby and the three men who waited there for him.

All of his thoughts had passed through his brain before he reached the ground floor. Scant weeks of memories that had seemed like a lifetime.

As Cash took those final steps, a pulse pounded at the side of his head. He dropped his flexing hand toward his holster and withdrew his six-shooter. He weighed the heft of it in his hand. The stiffness in his fingers concerned him.

He had reached the last step. He stood motionlessly for just a moment, bracing himself against the outer wall, considering what to do. Four bullets, against Steve and two of his fellow killers. He could turn that corner, expose himself with his gun blazing. If he was quick and his aim sure, he might be able to get off a few lucky shots or at least gun down Steve. Or he might leave himself an open target if they were prepared. He couldn't make the choice.

As if responding to a will outside himself, he simply turned the corner that opened into the lobby.

Steve Reno, The Whiskey Kid, had moved an armchair to the center of the lobby and was sitting in it, his legs crossed, facing the paneled partition from around which Cash had emerged. He was wearing the fancy cream-colored Stetson with the black band and smoking a cigarette, looking perfectly relaxed.

Slug Fletcher stood next to him, wearing his duster, his gun drawn and ready, and standing on Steve's other side was the cold-faced Andy Chelsea, likewise with a revolver in hand. Both of Steve Reno's boys regarded Cash with grim expressions. They meant business.

Cash walked forward. Steve wore a subtle smile.

He spoke brazenly. "If I knew 'bout where you was hidin' out, and if I knew 'bout you talkin' to the sheriff, surely you had to figger I'd know where you moved the girl. Just had to play my hunch this is where you'd run to."

Cash said nothing.

Steve pointed a finger at the Colt that Cash held at the ready.

"Think that's necessary, compadre?" he asked in a superficial tone of friendliness.

Cash was silent.

Steve settled back deeper into the thick upholstery of his chair. "If I recollect correctly, you only got four bullets in that gun."

"Might have reloaded," Cash said tonelessly.

Steve pushed his tongue into one cheek and shook his head. "Don't think so," he said, quietly confident.

"Don't matter how many shots I got. As long as I save one for you—compadre," Cash said with emphasis, though speaking with more assurance than he felt.

Steve was unthreatened. "You'll never get the chance," he said smugly.

Cash felt himself stiffening—from his own fear and with the rage that Steve had pushed back into him. But he couldn't expose any of what he was feeling to the three men. Steve in particular was searching him for just a crack of vulnerability.

Steve's tone became ominous. "We can make it easy or hard, Cash. We can ride out together or finish it here. Those are the only two choices you'll get."

All at once Cash felt a surge of confidence. He'd half expected the gunfire to erupt immediately. But Steve was acting in character, wanting to prolong this moment, still playing his game. He was comfortable in his position, felt he still held all the cards. That could give Cash the stall he needed. The few extra minutes for Garrett to arrive.

He had to keep Steve talking.

"What 'choices,' Steve? I'm a dead man either way."

"Yeah, you are," Steve confirmed. "But there's dyin' quick . . . and there's dyin' slow."

"Like what happened to Molly? Did she die slow? And what you did to my brother."

Steve nodded. "Yeah. Somethin' like that."

Cash braced himself before he said, "Took me all these years to find out what kind of a rat you are."

Steve looked impressed rather than angered. "Brave words. Could almost admire that comin' from a dead man."

Cash glanced at Slug, then Andy. Then his eyes returned to Steve.

"If *you* had any guts, you'd get rid of those two, and we'd go it alone," he said, challenging him.

Cash noticed the sudden tightening of Steve's facial muscles. He could see that he was pushing him. But he didn't want to go too far. Not yet. He needed just a little more time.

Steve regained his composure. He spoke with finality. "Last chance, Cash. Drop the gun, and make it easy on yourself. You don't wanna die here . . . not with your lady friend upstairs."

"And what happens to her?" Cash asked carefully.

Steve shrugged nonchalantly. "Nothin'. She ain't got nothin' to do with this."

Cash knew that Reno was lying. Just as he knew the second he pulled the trigger of his Colt, Slug or Andy would take him down. Steve had to know, though, that Cash's first bullet would be aimed at him. Yet he didn't seem concerned.

Then, out the corner of his eye, Cash saw the reason.

A form was creeping up on him from behind and just off to one side, emerging from behind the back corridor wall, his slow-moving, lamplit shadow just falling into Cash's peripheral view.

Cash kept his face expressionless.

And he reacted with suddenness.

He spun around and fired a shot at the approaching figure. He noticed in that instant that whoever the man was, he was wearing a glinting lawman's badge pinned to his chest. But to Cash's dismay, he didn't know if his bullet had hit its target, as the man swiftly dropped back out of sight behind the wall.

Slug and Andy Chelsea both began firing as Steve leaped out of his chair, knocking it over onto its side. His hand reached into his holster for his silver-mounted, pearl-handled Colt .45.

Cash threw himself back behind the protection of the wood-paneled partition. He pressed his body flat against the paneling just as the bullets whizzed by him. Then he twisted his upper torso slightly into the open and fired off a careless shot that went nowhere. He'd wasted another valuable bullet.

But he'd seen that Slug had rushed to Steve and was without cover. In the flash of a second, Cash's brain worked with razor-sharp clarity. He realized that unless he was precise with his aim, it would take more than a single bullet to bring down a man of Slug Fletcher's size. With only two bullets left in his Colt, he knew what he had to do and only hoped his aim was accurate and that his trigger finger didn't seize. He edged forward against the partition, revolver held firmly in his grip, then spun around, looking only for a brief instant into the fat, ugly features of Slug Fletcher, who himself saw the barrel of the Colt pointed directly at him. A lifetime of violence drained from Slug's face as Cash blasted a single, well-placed bullet into his brain, killing him instantly.

His move, however, had left him vulnerable to the aim of Andy Chelsea's gun.

Andy fired, and Cash caught the bullet, a searing punch in his gut. The impact spun him clear of his protective cover, and his body slammed back against the far wall, leaving him an open target. Next Steve's gun exploded, and Cash jerked upright with a slug in his shoulder, his gun arm dropping limply to his side. Both Steve and Andy converged on him while Cash struggled to raise his six-shooter.

With a sinking hopelessness, Cash knew it was over.

A scream suddenly distracted them. It was Lucinda, rushing down the last flight of stairs toward Cash.

"Lucinda! Stay back!" Cash yelled through his spit.

With Andy covering him, Steve rushed toward the staircase, just feet away from Cash, and pivoted to take aim at the girl. Cash took advantage of that moment to raise his Colt and fire his final bullet at Steve, catching him squarely in the side. Steve groaned and fell to his knees. But this action gave Andy Chelsea the opportunity to slam another slug into Cash's belly, at such close range that it ripped a bloody hole right through him, exiting out the flesh of his back and lodging in the wall. Cash gasped and slid slowly to the floor, smearing a red stain as he fell.

Then Andy turned his attention and directed his aim to the screaming Lucinda, who impulsively ran clear from the staircase toward Cash.

Cash was still conscious, but there was nothing he could do.

He closed his eyes and heard brief gunfire, and then the sound of a body thumping to the floor. He slowly opened his eyes . . . and saw Sheriff Garrett O'Dowd standing directly in front of him, smoke curling from the barrel of his revolver.

And he noticed that Andy Chelsea lay dead, facedown on his belly, with a deep stain of crimson blossoming across his back.

Lucinda dropped to her knees beside Cash and cradled him in her arms.

Garrett walked over to the still-kneeling Steve Reno and pulled the gun from his hand. Then he turned and spoke to an unseen presence.

"All right, Gilbert, show yourself. Hands raised high."

Garrett's deputy, Del Gilbert, nervously rounded the corner where he was hiding, arms stretched over his head. The sheriff went to him, clasped his hands behind his back, and slapped him into manacles. He then pushed him roughly into a chair. He turned to the visibly shaken desk clerk.

"Hurry and fetch Doc Pedersen," he ordered.

The desk clerk obeyed. "Right away. Yes, sir."

Garrett stepped over to Cash and Lucinda and knelt to a crouch. He cast a glance across at Del Gilbert. "Trusted deputy," he sneered. "In cahoots with Reno all along."

The sheriff then carefully lifted the front of Cash's shirt and examined the two belly wounds. While he wasn't a doctor, when he raised his face, his expression told all.

But he said to Cash, "I give you my word, Reno'll get the rope.

If not for the Overland, then . . ." Garrett lowered his eyes. He didn't have to say the rest.

"Think so?" Steve said, sweating and breathless but with his customary bravado, still on his knees and clutching at the wound in his side. "I was defendin' myself, Sheriff. Check McCall's gun."

Garrett turned his face toward Steve and gave an enigmatic smile. He took Cash's revolver from his hand, opened the cylinder, and shook out the four empty cartridges, which he then pocketed.

"You shot an unarmed man, Reno," he said smoothly. "That ain't self-defense."

The grin faded from Steve's face.

"When it comes time for trial, it'll be your word ag'in mine," Garrett said. He added with a slight yet triumphant smile, "And I'm a lawman."

Cash gazed into the tear-moistened eyes of Lucinda and through his pain managed a weak smile.

His voice was weak and his words faint. "Don't go feelin' sad, honey. We both knew it hadda end this way."

"No, Cash, don't say that, please," Lucinda pleaded, squeezing and massaging his arm. "The doctor's on his way. Everything can be all right now. Like we planned."

Cash held his eyes steady on the girl and maintained his smile—truthful with himself that, even with the strength and honesty of Lucinda's love, it wasn't enough.

And as he felt himself slip into a darkness from which he would not emerge, Cash McCall thought with comfort that his dying held no fear. Instead, his death brought with it a reward. In the fading moments of a life of lawlessness and regret, he had finally found redemption.

He was the last outlaw.